PREVIOUS BOOKS BY ALAN REFKIN

Fiction

Matt Moretti and Han Li Series
The Archivist
The Abductions
The Payback
The Forgotten
The Cabal

Mauro Bruno Detective Series
The Patriarch
The Scion
The Artifact
The Mistress

Gunter Wayan Series
The Organization
The Frame
The Arrangement

Nonfiction

The Wild Wild East: Lessons for Success in Business in Contemporary Capitalist China
By Alan Refkin and Daniel Borgia, PhD

Doing the China Tango: How to Dance around Common Pitfalls in Chinese Business Relationships
By Alan Refkin and Scott Cray

Conducting Business in the Land of the Dragon: What Every Businessperson Needs To Know About China
By Alan Refkin and Scott Cray

Piercing the Great Wall of Corporate China: How to Perform Forensic Due Diligence on Chinese Companies
By Alan Refkin and David Dodge

THE
CHASE

A MATT MORETTI & HAN LI THRILLER

ALAN REFKIN

THE CHASE
A MATT MORETTI & HAN LI THRILLER

iUniverse books may be ordered through booksellers or by contacting:

iUniverse
1663 Liberty Drive
Bloomington, IN 47403
www.iuniverse.com
844-349-9409

Because of the dynamic nature of the Internet, any web addresses or links contained in this book may have changed since publication and may no longer be valid. The views expressed in this work are solely those of the author and do not necessarily reflect the views of the publisher, and the publisher hereby disclaims any responsibility for them.

Any people depicted in stock imagery provided by Getty Images are models, and such images are being used for illustrative purposes only.
Certain stock imagery © Getty Images.

ISBN: 978-1-6632-4622-6 (sc)
ISBN: 978-1-6632-4623-3 (e)

Library of Congress Control Number: 2022918523

Print information available on the last page.

iUniverse rev. date: 10/04/2022

To my wife, Kerry
To Scott Cray

ACKNOWLEDGMENTS

Scott Cray, to whom this book is dedicated, is my co-author on two business books relating to China—*Doing the China Tango: How to Dance around Common Pitfalls in Chinese Business Relationships* and *Conducting Business in the Land of the Dragon: What Every Businessperson Needs To Know About China.* A close friend, he has a straightforward and honest way of looking at a situation, which I tried to emulate in Lieutenant Colonel Douglas Cray. For decades, he and his wife Betty have conducted many charitable activities, lifting the lives of those who virtually have nothing and giving them a ray of sunshine. Betty is also an accomplished author, having written *Finding Joy...after Foreclosure: The Unlikely Adoption of an Old Dalmatian.* It will bring tears to your eyes.

To: Kerry Refkin, who has fantastic insights on the storyline and works with the amazing cover design talents at iUniverse to produce the perfect cover for my novels.

To: My editor, a heartfelt thank you for your valuable comments that made my story more compelling.

Go to alanrefkin.com for photos of me at many of the locations mentioned in the novel. *Story Settings* will let you see the referenced venues, weapons, aircraft, ships, etc.

CHAPTER
ONE

The Eduardo Gomes International Airport in Manaus, Brazil, was nine hundred miles from the country's Atlantic coast and in the heart of the rainforest. Situated along the north bank of the Negro River, eleven miles above its influx into the Amazon River, the Amazon Basin's largest urban area had a population of over one million eight hundred thousand. The city was a popular staging area for tourist companies offering cruises on the mighty river for those who wanted to see rainforests and the jungle's natural beauty from their boat. For the more adventurous, shore excursions offered an opportunity to walk through the rainforest. However, with humidity that averaged between seventy-seven and eighty-eight percent, the air felt like it was one hundred degrees even when the temperature was in the mid-eighties. When the outside temperature reached ninety, it felt a furnace-like one hundred twenty degrees. Therefore, many passengers elected to remain onboard and view the jungle from afar.

Lieutenant Colonel Douglas Cray's commercial flight landed in Manaus on schedule and he passed through customs and immigration without issue. The six feet tall, one hundred seventy pounds former Army Ranger intelligence officer had sandy brown hair, blue eyes, a slight Bostonian accent, and a jogger's physique. That slenderness and accent made the thirty-nine-year-old appear to be a college professor rather than the stereotypical bulked-up ground-pounder image most had of special forces members.

His current position was the administrative head of Nemesis. This joint United States-China off-the-books organization operated outside the slow-moving bureaucracies that plagued both nations and had a mandate to eliminate critical threats to both countries. Named after the Greek goddess for retribution against evil deeds, only thirteen people knew of Nemesis' existence.

At President Ballinger's insistence, Cray had been told to take time off and leave Washington so he couldn't work from home while recovering from a sniper's bullet. Therefore, since this trip had been a last-minute decision, he had not been able to leave Washington in time to arrive in Manaus before his cruise ship sailed. This problem wasn't unique, and the booking agent had offered for an additional fee to put him on a floatplane charter that would take him to his vessel, the Selva, while it was en route. Now, following the information he had received, he was met in the arrivals area by a driver who took him to the floatplane company.

It was eight miles from the airport to the Port of Manaus. When he arrived, he saw a floatplane alongside a dock where the pilot was performing a preflight check. Walking into the company's office, which was a thirty-by-thirty-foot room with a counter along the back wall and a few chairs to the left of it, he was unprepared for the heated argument that was taking place between the agent and an attractive woman.

"I can't wait until tomorrow. This is the only charter left on the river. Whatever the person who hired your aircraft is paying, I'll pay triple it in cash."

The woman arguing with the agent was five feet, seven inches tall, tan, had long blonde hair, an athletic physique, and soft blue eyes. Cray believed she usually got her way because of her natural beauty. This looked to be the exception.

Seeing Cray walk into the office, the agent held up his index finger to signal he'd be with him momentarily while continuing to explain to the woman that the aircraft she wanted wasn't available. That triggered her transition from assertive to bitch mode, demanding to speak with the company's owner. Ignoring her request, which by the expression on her face ratcheted up her irritation, the agent summoned Cray forward and, after greeting him, asked for his passport, which he presented.

"I'll pay triple what you paid if you let me take your charter," the woman said with a New York accent, taking a position between Cray and the agent. "He says the floatplane is available tomorrow. Delay your trip by a day and walk away with a free charter and a pile of cash."

"I'm not interested."

"Listen, whatever your name is—."

"Doug Cray."

"Erin Sanders. I must photograph an area of jungle that loggers are illegally clearing, and I need those photos in the magazine editor's hands by the end of the day to make the printing deadline."

"Plan better."

"This was a last-minute assignment given to me because I just finished another photo shoot in Rio."

"Do you work for a magazine in New York City?" Cray asked, guessing where she was from by her accent.

"I'm an independent photographer. This assignment was from a magazine headquartered in the Big Apple."

"Do you live there?"

"In a loft in Tribecca," she answered, dialing down her attitude.

"What happens if you don't get the photos?"

"Without photos, the magazine's article will have the impact of a spitball hitting a wall. People may not read the article, but they'll look at the pictures. The editor is hoping they'll create a fury among environmentalists and the Brazilian people that will force government officials, who either turned a blind eye to the problem or accepted bribes from the loggers, to step in and protect their forests from being raped and thousands of animals from becoming homeless or killed. I want to catch them cutting down trees and show them denuding the land."

"Maybe there's a way to satisfy both our needs. Can you tell or show the agent where you need to go?"

She removed a map from her bag and pointed to the area.

"It's two hours from here, maybe a little less," the agent said.

"If we fly to her destination first, how far is it from there to my boat?" Cray asked.

"The Selva has a rainforest shore excursion today, and it should be in this area," the agent answered, tapping his finger at a point on the map. "That's approximately an hour from here and two from where she wants to go. Four hours flying time for you."

"I've already paid for the charter. What if she also pays you the charter fee? We go to the logging site, she takes her photos, and then the pilot brings me to the Selva and returns her here."

"If she pays double the charter fee, I'll modify your charter," the agent answered.

The woman placed the cash on the counter and struck the deal.

The three walked to the aircraft.

"Nasty fall?" Sanders asked, seeing Cray pulling his roller bag with his left hand while using a cane with his right.

"Something like that."

When they arrived at the plane, the pilot, who Cray was relieved to hear spoke English, took Cray's bag and put it in the rear storage bay along with Sanders' carryon. The agent then told him about the change in the itinerary, with Sanders showing the aviator on the map where she wanted to go and what she was going to photograph.

"No problem, the pilot said. "I was born in Manaus and spent the last three decades flying Amazon charters out of the city. It should be easy to take you there and put the floatplane into a slip where the aircraft moves sideways as well as forward. That will give you a better view of the loggers."

"Where do you want us to sit?" Cray asked.

When the pilot didn't immediately respond, based on past flights in small planes, Cray realized he must be doing a quick weight and balance calculation in his head.

"In the two rear seats," the he finally responded.

Cray and Sanders strapped themselves in and watched as the pilot climbed into the cockpit and latched the door.

The engine started smoothly, after which the pilot slowly maneuvered the floatplane into the center of the river and pushed the throttle to full power. As the plane gained speed, he applied back pressure until it rose, then gradually released it and let the aircraft sail across the water as if on a pair of skis. As he approached takeoff speed, he used his ailerons to lift the left float, which reduced aerodynamic drag and allowed the aircraft to accelerate to its best climbing speed. Two thousand three hundred forty-one feet later, the plane was airborne.

After leaving the Negro River, the thirty year old aircraft leveled out at fifteen hundred feet and started across the dense Amazon jungle. Several times during the flight, Sanders requested the pilot put the plane into a slip so she could snap a series of photos, which she later told Cray would serve as a sharp contrast to the deforested area she believed they'd see.

An hour and fifty minutes after takeoff, the pilot turned his head towards the rear of the aircraft and spoke to Sanders. "The spot on the map that you pointed to is just ahead."

The contrast was stark. One instant they were looking at dense jungle, the next they were flying over vacant land in New Mexico. At the edge of this clearing, there was a line of logging trucks waiting to be loaded with the illegal cuttings from the dozen workers wielding chainsaws near to them. Establishing a perimeter around them were men wielding automatic rifles. The pilot put the plane into a slip, and Sanders took photograph after photograph.

A floatplane isn't quiet—the relic that Cray and Sanders were in being especially noisy. The perimeter security team heard the aircraft before seeing it, upon which they sent hundreds of rounds at the low-moving museum piece to try and bring it down. None hit the plane because it was farther away than it appeared. However, the pilot's eyes widened, and his mouth went slightly agape upon seeing the muzzle flashes.

"Those guns have an effective range of around six hundred yards," Cray said. "They can't hit you."

The pilot turned and looked at him as if he was on drugs.

"I'm US military, and I know my weapons. They'll need something bigger than what they're holding to hit us."

The pilot, who had never before had someone shooting at his plane, began sweating and looked ready to bolt from the area. Sensing what was about to happen, Sanders dug into her camera bag, removed the last of her cash, about three hundred dollars, and leaned forward and stuffed it into his shirt pocket. That didn't calm the pilot, but it incentivized him to stay in the area. Despite what Cray said, he increased his altitude by twelve hundred feet and began circling the loggers, the plane remaining untouched despite a continuous series of muzzle flashes.

Sanders took numerous photos of loggers cutting down trees, trucks hauling the wood away, and the stark contrast between the recently denuded area with the dense forest behind it.

"Thanks, I have what I need. We can leave," she said after fifteen minutes of circling.

The pilot didn't need to be told twice and left the area, banking the plane steeply as he changed direction and started across the jungle.

"When will we return to Manaus?" she asked.

"It's two hours to the boat. If it's where I think it is, it'll be one hour from there to the dock."

Sanders looked at her watch. "That gives me enough time to meet my deadline."

Forty-five minutes after they left the logging area, they saw a Sikorsky UH-60 Black Hawk—a four-blade, sixty-five feet long twin-engine helicopter, come out of nowhere and parallel them on the pilot's side of the plane.

"That's a Brazilian Air Force aircraft," the pilot said, seeing the bright yellow insignia on the side, which displayed a sword in front of a pair of wings.

"What do they want?" Cray asked.

The pilot said he didn't know after failing to get an answer from the helicopter's pilot on the guard frequency.

Thirty seconds later, Cray's question got answered when the Black Hawk's side door slid open, revealing an older person in uniform aiming a large, mounted machine gun at the floatplane. The pilot, who wasn't going to ask the intentions of the person aiming the gun, immediately put the floatplane into a steep dive—bringing it within a gnat's whisker of the jungle canopy. He then zigzagged across the jungle, hoping the Black Hawk's pilot wasn't crazy enough to follow because the jungle canopy wasn't of equal height and, at their altitude and speed, a tree branch less than a foot higher than its neighbor could bring them down. With only seat belts, Cray and Sanders held onto the lift handles beside their heads during the aircraft's gyrations, attempting to keep from smashing into one another and the seats in front of them.

"We need to keep a thousand feet away from that gun," Sanders shouted to the pilot, who was focusing on the jungle canopy and either ignored or didn't hear her.

"That's a Browning .50 caliber machine gun, and it has a range of two thousand yards," Cray said. "Each round has enough energy to go through both sides of this aircraft, and anything in between, like a hot knife through butter."

"Can we outrun the helicopter?"

"Not a Black Hawk. Those I've been in had a speed of around two hundred twenty mph, and I don't think we can get close to that speed with the drag from our floats."

The helicopter had been following the floatplane from a distance as the pilot zigzagged across the jungle. However, that changed when it sped up and positioned itself fifty yards from the pilot's side of the plane. As Cray predicted, the first round from the Browning, traveling at two thousand nine hundred ten feet per second, or one thousand nine hundred eighty-four mph, effortlessly went through the aircraft's thin aluminum siding and struck the pilot in the third vertebrosterno rib. That bone exploded into multiple shards and sent a fatal barrage of fragments into his heart. Simultaneously, the shockwave from the heavy round's kinetic energy produced a cavity within his body which compressed the flesh around it and crushed every vital organ. Upon exiting the body, the bullet punched through the plane's starboard side and fell into the jungle.

Because the aircraft was virtually on top of the jungle canopy and trimmed downward to help keep it low at full power, when the pilot died the control column released from his grip and the plane nosed sharply down, instantly striking the canopy of a two hundred feet high and ten feet in diameter kapok tree. The aircraft's tail and wings sheared at impact. As the airframe continued downward, its momentum and weight continually hitting the tree's branches finally took their toll, and the cockpit broke away from the fuselage. The rest of the airframe continued its descent, slowing as it bounced off the thinner lower branches, as if it were a steel ball in a pachinko machine, until it impacted the thick bed of ferns surrounding the tree.

Cray and Sanders were in a fog from the impact and took a few seconds to pull it together. He was the first to recover and, smelling kerosene and feeling liquid raining on him from above, realized it came from aviation fuel leaking from the broken wings. "We need to get out of these seats," he said to Sanders, reaching to his right and unfastening her seat belt, grimacing in pain from his wound as he did.

"I broke my left collarbone," she said, crying in pain as he helped her from her seat. Once out of the wreckage, she pulled back the top of her blouse, exposing a bulge on her shoulder.

"Move your arm."

When she did, there was a grinding sound and intense pain. "It's broken," he confirmed. Taking off his undershirt, he made a sling to immobilize it by keeping the arm close to her body.

"Thanks. What happened to you?" she asked, noticing the bandage when he removed his undershirt.

"Someone shot me. The doctors said it'll take six months to heal if I don't aggravate the wound."

"You blew that."

"I had some help."

Both returned their focus to the present.

"When will someone come looking for us?" Sanders asked.

"It may be some time. Since we were the company's last charter, there was no reason for the clerk or anyone else to stick around and wait for our return. They may not know we're missing until tomorrow morning. But that's not the worst part."

"You're not helping my anxiety. What could be worse than waiting until morning for a search team?"

"Remember when the pilot told us he'd flown this jungle for thirty years?"

"Yes."

"When you told him where you wanted to go, I didn't see him look at a navigational chart to plot a course to the logging camp."

"Neither did I."

"I'm guessing that's because he's flown over the Amazon jungle so often that he flies by habit using local landmarks, which we can't discern because everything in the jungle looks the same to us. He also apparently has a habit of flying close to the jungle canopy."

"Is that the worst part?"

"Not yet. We were too low to be on radar, and without the pilot filing a flight plan, rescue aircraft would have thousands of square miles of jungle to search because no one would know what route we took or where we went down. Even if a rescue team flies over this area, they won't see the wreckage because it's below the dense tree canopy. In the Amazon, spotting it would be like locating a glass bottle in the ocean. I have a satphone in my luggage—which was either jettisoned from the wreckage or is two hundred feet above us in a tree whose branches start sixty feet off the jungle floor."

Sanders started hyperventilating, and her hands trembled. "If that's not the worst part, I'm not feeling well," she said.

"You're having an anxiety attack. Slow your breathing, take deep breaths, and focus on my face."

She did, the trembling in her hands and her rapid breathing gradually subsiding. "Is the worst part that we'll die without food or water?"

"I'm an ex-Army Ranger who's had extensive survival training. Finding food and water in the jungle is not our biggest challenge."

"What is the worst part?"

"To avoid becoming the next meal for the apex predators around us."

CHAPTER
TWO

Colonel Thiago Vilar was forty-two years old, stood five feet eight inches tall, weighed one hundred eighty-five pounds, and had a round face with close-cropped black hair and a mustache to the edge of his upper lip. In command of rotary aircraft within the Aviation Group of the Brazilian Air Force, headquartered in Brasilia, he was operationally responsible for every military helicopter within the country.

He was returning to Manaus Air Force Base after shooting down the floatplane that Samuel Bradford, the FBI's Executive Assistant Director for Intelligence, paid him to destroy. They communicated by Tor, a secure encrypted protocol that ensured privacy for data and communications on the web through a series of layered nodes that hid IP addresses and browsing history. According to an NSA briefing that Bradford received, this system was unbreakable.

The intel director was five feet nine inches in height, slender but not thin, clean-shaven, and had his black hair styled in a conservative taper cut. He was vain about his appearance, with his teeth regularly whitened and his body spray tanned every ten days at his plastic surgeon's office—the physician having tightened his neck, arms, and anything else that sagged.

Bradford's instructions stipulated that the crash receive zero publicity. Although Vilar's assignments from the intel officer were infrequent, the stipend to his offshore account for each task was equivalent to five years of military pay. Therefore, he was eager to do whatever was required to get paid.

The colonel realized these off-the-books assignments came with the risk of discovery. However, he considered this exposure small since he brought down a private aircraft flying over the Amazon Basin. While the plane would be visible on ATC radar, he'd avoid detection by ordering his pilot to fly below it.

Because he knew the approximate time Cray's charter was to leave the Manaus dock and its destination would be the Selva, he positioned the Black Hawk to intercept the floatplane midway there, believing the pilot would follow the river because it was the shortest route to the boat. Bringing the aircraft down in the rainforest meant there was virtually no chance of discovery. However, his plan went out the window when the plane was a no-show. That necessitated doing something he wanted to avoid, which was to call air traffic control, a system that was functionally under the auspices of the military.

The reason for avoiding contact with ATC was that there would be a record of his inquiry. If someone over whom he had no control looked into the floatplane's disappearance, that inquiry would be a red flag to the investigator. He didn't expect that to happen, but why take the chance? However, in this situation, he had no choice. He called ATC and asked if they had on their screen a plane that left the Manaus dock around the time he gave them. Unsurprisingly, they responded by giving him the floatplane's coordinates and altitude.

Because the floatplane wasn't close to their current position, and he'd been airborne for some time waiting to ambush it, Vilar had no choice but to go to Manaus Air Force Base to refuel before going after it. That was a painful decision because he didn't know if the floatplane would get to its destination and drop off its passenger before he could kill him. But he had no choice.

The refueling went quickly, and once the Black Hawk approached the coordinates ATC originally gave him, Vilar called for an update, resulting in a slight course correction that pinpointed the floatplane.

Knowing that ATC would see the aircraft suddenly drop off the radar wasn't a concern because charters flew low over the rainforest to give their passengers a closer view and sometimes landed on one of the tributaries that cut through the jungle. The concern came if the pilot radioed they had a problem, or the aircraft was overdue in reaching its destination.

When Vilar landed at Manaus, he sent a message to Bradford, telling him the charter flight crashed in the jungle with no sign of survivors, adding the man he was to kill was sitting next to a woman. He next needed to ensure that this crash received no publicity if, as expected, the charter company reported the plane was missing. He made this happen by calling the editors of the country's four major newspapers—*O Globo, Jornal do Brasil, O Estado de Sao Paulo, and Folha de Sao Paulo.* All fed their bylines to Brazil's six hundred fifty smaller daily publications. The story he told them was that a small aircraft went down over the Amazon, and the government, for national security reasons, didn't want to advertise who was onboard. In a democratic society, that revelation would create the same frenzy as pouring blood into a pool of sharks. However, since there was a history of people who went against the wishes of the government disappearing, each of the editors took his admonitions seriously and vowed not to pursue the story nor mention it in their digital or print media.

At the Manaus Air Force Base, Vilar got into an Airbus C-295 transport aircraft for the twelve-hundred-mile flight to Brasilia. Because the floatplane went down in an unexplored area of the jungle where the wreckage and bodies would be impossible to see under a dense jungle canopy, no one would believe that what occurred was anything but a catastrophic mechanical problem. With the pilot and passengers sure to be devoured by jungle predators eager for a protein meal, what happened would forever be a mystery. He was wrong.

When he arrived in Brasilia, he read an email from Bradford that said to message him when he returned to his office. He did. The two then began an exchange, with Bradford writing he was unsatisfied with Vilar's previous message and curious about the identity of the woman with Cray. However, he assumed she was another cruise ship passenger. He explained his dissatisfaction stemmed from the Brazilian colonel's failure to see a body.

"Why couldn't you see a body?" Bradford typed.

"The jungle is very dense; you can't see the ground if you're above the tree canopies."

"Until I have photographic confirmation of his death, I consider him to be alive."

"No one survives a crash in the Amazon jungle."

"An assumption that I can't afford to make. Do you have a search team who doesn't ask questions?"

"I have access to a military squad specializing in sensitive operations."

"Send them to look for survivors. There won't be any."

"I understand and will make that clear."

The charter company clerk was in a panic. Standing beside the dock and looking skyward in the direction in which the floatplane always made its approach, he'd smoked an endless series of cigarettes until the pack was empty. Since it was almost dark, a time after which the plane couldn't land on the river because of the lack of lighting and the trickiness of the approach, which required a steep descent after clearing a tall grove of trees at the bend in the river, he knew something happened to the aircraft. Several unanswered calls to the pilot on their company frequency, and a call to the Selva's purser verifying the plane hadn't yet arrived, fortified that belief. This brought back memories of what occurred six years earlier when the previous owner and pilot of the charter business failed to return. Because the aircraft didn't file a flight plan, government search teams had no idea where it could be within Brazil's one million six hundred thousand square miles of the Amazon Basin. Therefore, they launched only a token search to satisfy those who harbored unrealistic expectations that it was possible to find the aircraft and passengers and expect them to be alive. Months later, his current employer bought the business from the pilot's widow. He expected the same to happen this time, but he wasn't going to stick around and wait for that to occur.

He returned to his office, put his items in a box, hung a sign on the door in Portuguese that the business was closed, and went home. He didn't bother to call the government to organize a search knowing that it was a worthless pursuit without the approximate crash location. Just as before, they'd go through the motions without expecting success.

The following day the clerk applied for a job at the Eduardo Gomes International Airport as an airport luggage dispatcher and was given a job on the spot because of his charter aircraft experience. As he predicted, two days after her husband failed to return, the pilot's wife put the charter company up for sale.

The Brazilian Army, referred to as the Exército Brasileiro within Latin America, had seven commands—one of which was the Twelfth Military Region, or Amazon Military Command, which handled the defense of the Amazon Basin. The twelfth had an assigned troop strength of twenty-six thousand three hundred, with their training singularly focused on jungle warfare. The commander of the twelfth, and Vilar's counterpart, was Colonel Henrique Rocha—a graduate of the Academia Militar das Agulhas Negras, the country's most distinguished military academy, established in 1792. The forty-year-old was six feet, one inch tall, a muscular one hundred eighty-eight pounds, had a ramrod straight posture, and was bald since his late twenties because of a genetic trait from his mother. His light brown skin matched the color of his eyes. If there were boots on the ground in the Amazon Basin, they were under his command.

Rocha had previously done business with Vilar helping drug smugglers, human traffickers, and corporations who needed to keep locals in line when they denuded or polluted their property. In performing these services, they depended on the squad commanded by Captain Reinaldo Torres because those within it had no morals, were only interested in the money they'd receive, and kept their mouths shut. Vilar told Rocha what he wanted, and that time was of the essence. Once he negotiated the fee, the call ended with him providing the crash site coordinates and the name of the person to be photographed.

Rocha looked at a map of the Amazon Basin, found the coordinates, and stared. It was the earthly equivalent of a black hole in space—an area for which no maps or hard information existed as to what lay within—only conjecture.

Taking the headset off the cradle of his desktop phone, he pressed the button that connected him to the commander of the Sixteenth Jungle Infantry Brigade in Tefé, which was two hundred seventy-eight miles west of Manaus. He ordered him to send Torres' squad to the coordinates he provided to search for plane crash survivors, ending their conversation by saying that this was a top-secret mission that he couldn't discuss with anyone but him.

The commander of the Sixteenth, looking as he spoke at a large map of the Amazon Basin that extended across the entire rear wall of his office, put his finger on the coordinates and shook his head in disbelief.

"Is there a problem?" Rocha asked when the line went silent.

"The coordinates are in the Vale do Javari," the commander said, referring to an area the size of Austria where the Brazilian government prohibited non-indigenous people from entering because of the extreme danger it posed to the uninvited. "More than a dozen groups I know ignored this entry prohibition and never came back. The tribes there are very territorial and kill intruders; at least one is known to be headhunters."

Rocha ignored the admonitions. "Have the captain call me as soon as possible," Rocha said, ending the call without further discussion.

Torres was a grizzled veteran who grew up in Santarem, a city east of Manaus where the Tapajós River meets the Amazon. He was five feet five inches tall with light brown skin, hazel-colored eyes, close-cropped brown hair, and the body of a weightlifter—which resulted from his daily routine of working out with weights. He had a no-nonsense attitude and no sense of humor. Upon arriving at the commander's office, he received his assignment and told it was top secret. That didn't come as a surprise because he'd already spoken to Rocha. His meeting with the commander was to give him the illusion that he was directing a search and rescue operation.

"The Javari Valley," Torres said, the look on his face reflecting the same uneasiness he displayed when speaking with Rocha.

"If the crash coordinates are accurate, you won't have to go far. It'll be a quick in and out."

"Let's hope so."

"It's too dangerous to insert at this time of day. You leave in the morning. If I don't hear from you for two days, I'll assume your squad is in trouble."

"This is the Javari Valley. If you don't hear from me in two days, we'll be dead."

CHAPTER
THREE

ray and Sanders agreed they had an extremely low probability of being rescued if they remained with the wreckage. Because the pilot flew inches above the jungle canopy, well below ATC radar, and zigzagged across the rainforest, no one would have any idea where they crashed.

"The Amazon River has over eleven hundred tributaries," Cray said, repeating what he'd read when preparing for his cruise. "There will be settlements along or near them because everything living in this environment, man or beast, needs water to survive."

"How do we find a settlement?"

"Since we don't know where the tributaries are, much less the settlements, it'll be a matter of luck."

"You're supposed to be reassuring. Did you flunk sensitivity training in the Army?"

"We're trained to recognize reality. But if we have a shot at finding a tributary or settlement, we need to go in that direction," he said, pointing to his left.

She gave him a questioning look.

"That's where the jungle floor is sloping downward. Because gravity pulls water to a lower elevation, if we follow the gradual descent of the land, we have a shot at finding a tributary. However, I don't know how far it will be."

"Tell me you were at the top of your class in survival training."

"Graduated dead last and spent my career as a Ranger intelligence officer. Never saw a jungle again."

"Terrific."

As they silently walked through the jungle, the trauma from the crash, fatigue, and injuries increasingly took their toll. Cray's limp worsened, and even though he hadn't told Sanders, a constant throbbing pain came from his wound. Sanders was similarly non-talkative about her injury. Because they were walking, her arm was never wholly immobile, even with the homemade sling. Her broken clavicle hurt like hell, the pain elevating to excruciating when she stumbled over the uneven jungle floor.

Cray held the cane with his left hand. In his right, he had an improvised weapon—a four feet long, narrow piece of aluminum tubing salvaged from the wreckage. One end had a sharp, jagged edge which he felt might be helpful for defense. It wasn't much of a weapon, but it was all he could find in the piece of aircraft which hit the ground. Sanders carried a three feet long section of tubing in her right hand. Just as with Cray's, one end was jagged where it'd torn free of the fuselage. She slung her camera bag over her right shoulder.

"Stop!" Cray yelled.

Sanders, who was to his left, immediately complied. She looked for a threat but didn't see any. "What?" she asked in a scared voice.

He pointed with his cane to a pile of leaves five feet in front of her. "Leaves don't move unless there's a breeze," he said. Bending down, he put his cane on the ground and picked up a small stone. He then threw it at the pile. When it hit, a seven feet long snake, with a dorsal pattern of X-shaped markings on a brownish background, darted from beneath the leaves and into the jungle brush.

Sanders screamed; her eyes locked on the retreating snake.

"That was a Bushmaster, and it's very poisonous," Cray said matter-of-factly as he picked up his cane.

"Does it have family members in that pile?"

Cray stepped forward and prodded the leaves with the aluminum

19

tubing but got no response. "It was hunting alone. Most snakes will stay away from us, preferring to go after smaller prey. They usually strike only when threatened."

"Usually?"

"I'm not a snake psychologist."

Above them, they could hear the rain pelting the tops of the surrounding trees, accompanied by thunder. Very little precipitation came through the dense, interlocking layers of branches and leaves.

"It's raining hard above us," Sanders said, looking up as she did.

"Unless it's a monsoon-like storm, we won't get drenched, but the increased humidity the rain creates makes it hard to stay dry. Our clothes, hair, and body will always stay moist, just as they are now."

"Too bad we can't get that water down here. I'm parched."

"Me too. Let's have a drink," Cray said, going to a tree entangled with vines. Using the edge of his tubing, he cut deeply into a vine, saw the liquid dripping from it was clear, and motioned for her to join him. "Open your mouth," he said. As she did, he tilted the slit vine, and the liquid dropped gently into it. Once she'd had enough, he cut open another vine and took his fill.

"Do all jungle vines have water?"

"As a general rule, those with rough bark and shoots over an inch and a half in diameter usually do. However, those that have a milky sap instead of clear liquid are poisonous. You also don't want to suck on the vines but let the liquid drip into your mouth because their exterior can sometimes irritate the lips."

"How far do you think we walked?"

"A mile, maybe a mile and a quarter. Since it's getting late, we need to find a place where we can construct a shelter for the night, build a fire, and get something to eat."

"Why not keep pushing while it's daylight? We can eat later."

"If we don't find shelter and build a fire, we'll be the main course for the seventy to ninety percent of jungle predators living in the surrounding trees," he said.

"Oh."

The site Cray picked was a fallen tree which, hit by lightning, snapped—the top resting on the ground while the bottom was loosely attached four feet from the base. Checking under the trunk for snakes, tarantulas, and anything else that might harm them, they evicted a half dozen giant centipedes—ten-inch-long poisonous insects whose bite caused severe pain. Afterward, they collected dry leaves and other debris which would be their bed and insulated them from the moist jungle floor.

They next focused on building a fire, beginning by gathering large and small twigs, rotted branches, and dry fungus and leaves—the latter serving as tinder. To start the fire, Cray found a thick piece of bark beside the fallen tree and a short section of a broken branch around three-eighths of an inch in diameter. He used the jagged aluminum tubing to gouge a V-shaped notch in the bark and smooth the thick twig so that it rolled easily between his hands.

As he was doing this, Sanders gave him a look that showed she was on edge. "It's getting dark. From what you said, the dinner bell will soon sound for the predators in these trees."

"I'm almost there," Cray replied as he walked to a pile of rotted branches and, making several trips, placed half the stack five feet on either side of the fallen tree. Kneeling, he took the notched bark and smooth twig in hand. "When you see smoke coming from the bark, place a small amount of the fungus on it, but not too much," Cray said as he rapidly rubbed the smooth twig between his palms, moving his hands up and down it as he did. It wasn't long before the friction between the twig and bark created smoke and flecks of fire.

"Now," Cray told Sanders, who added tinder to the infant flame as he blew lightly on it. Within a few seconds, it ignited, and he took the bark to the stack of rotten branches and dumped the tinder onto it. The branches ignited. Once the fire got going, he brought a burning branch to the pile of wood on the other side of their shelter and started that fire.

"That should keep us safe," Sanders said.

"Safe? No. It'll repel some nocturnal species because their eyes are always in low light, and the fire causes pain or hampers their vision. Other predators will associate fire with humans and stay away from us. However, most apex predators don't care about campfires. They're hungry and won't let it hamper getting something to eat."

"How do we avoid them?"

"If one approaches, jab it as hard as possible with the sharp end of the metal tube. That may inflict enough pain so it'll move on and find easier prey. That's our only defense."

"What about hitting it with a burning piece of wood?"

"We could try, but if we're close enough to do that, we'll be close enough for it to kill us."

"Why am I not feeling good about us making it through the night?"

"You shouldn't."

"Changing the subject," she said abruptly, "any idea how we can get a last meal? I'm famished."

"If we survive the night, in the morning, I'll bring you breakfast in bed, so to speak."

"That's hard to believe."

"But true. Until then, staying alive will be a challenge. We'll sleep in shifts so that one of us is always awake and keeping the fires going. I'll take the first shift."

High above them, the Amazon's largest apex predator was watching his next meal. There were other predators in surrounding trees, but none would move until the jaguar claimed its meal. Once it did, they'd find another source of food because trying to share the top apex predator's meal would make them an additional course.

The jaguar watching Cray and Sanders' encampment weighed three hundred pounds, displayed pale yellow fur covered by spots that transitioned to rosettes on the sides, and as with all Amazonian jaguars, had an unusually powerful bite of fifteen hundred pounds per square inch. This allowed it to bite through its victim's skull—its preferred method of killing. The carnivore depended solely on flesh for survival and could take down prey of equal weight. Blessed with excellent night vision, since that's when it hunted, its eyes locked on its target as it quietly descended from its lofty perch atop the kapok tree.

Cray saw how haggard Sanders looked and planned to stay awake until it was almost daylight to let her get as much sleep as possible. Deep in thought trying to recall what he had learned in jungle survival school; he never heard the jaguar set foot on the jungle floor. One instant there was nothing and the next it was between him and the fire. While he recalled from his training the dimensions of a jaguar, that didn't prepare him for the enormity of the creature standing three feet tall at the shoulder and slightly over six feet in length that was fearlessly watching him. His heartbeat went into overdrive on seeing it and the predator's indifference to the fire.

He looked the giant cat in the eyes, trying not to show fear which, he had been told, would cause a predator to attack immediately. While staring at it, he slowly extended his left arm to grab his weapon. Given the massive size of the animal, he thought that hurting it enough so that it would run away was like a Hail Mary pass in football. Sometimes it worked, but most of the time, it didn't.

As he slowly extended his hand to get his weapon, he failed to find it and grasped dry leaves instead. He couldn't afford to turn his head and look for it, believing that breaking eye contact would communicate fear and invite an immediate attack. As the Jaguar cautiously approached and bared its teeth, there were sudden flashes of light, identical to what one might see in a lightning storm but without the sound. Sensing danger, the carnivore retreated to its kapok tree and ascended it until enveloped by darkness. When it was out of sight, Cray turned around and saw Sanders holding her camera with the flash atop it.

"That was quick thinking. I thought you were asleep."

"I got up to go to the bathroom, taking my camera to get a shot of our camp for my scrapbook should we survive. When I saw the jaguar, I thought about using the flash to make it appear as if it were lightning."

"Given its size, our weapons wouldn't have stopped it," Cray said, seeing his metal tube was a foot to the left of where he reached.

"Thanks for saving my life."

"How else was I going to get breakfast."

Cray woke Sanders not long after sunlight hit the jungle floor, placing in front of her an assortment of fruits displayed on an immature three feet long *Coccoloba gigantifolia* leaf from the Brazilian tree that grew leaves eight feet long.

"This is amazing," she said, looking at the fruits.

"I only picked those with which I was familiar. I tried each to make sure none were poisonous. As I'm still vertical, I think I succeeded."

That brought a laugh.

"I packed fruit to take with us," he said before leaving their shelter and returning with two bark containers.

"You made the containers?"

"It didn't take any time at all once I found a young tree with loose bark. I took my anti-jaguar weapon, peeled bark off this fallen tree, and scratched the shape I wanted into it. I wrapped pieces of vines around the bark to hold everything together."

"There are even straps for you to carry them. Are you sure you finished last in your survival class?"

"Positive."

CHAPTER
FOUR

At dawn, a Black Hawk helicopter carrying Torres and seven members of his team left Tefé. Because of the dense rainforest canopy cover, they didn't expect to see the crash site from the air. Therefore, they planned to descend to the jungle floor, find the wreckage, and photograph the corpses—whether they died in the crash or from their encounter with his team. Afterward, they'd request an extraction transport.

Although they expected this to be an in and out, searching for anything within the jungle doesn't always go as planned because of the difficulty with establishing outside communications, getting GPS fixes, the denseness of the trees and vegetation, and the need to move slowly to avoid deadly reptiles, carnivores, arachnids, and other creatures that could kill with a single bite. Therefore, Torres' team packed three days of supplies in their backpacks. If the search took longer, they'd live off whatever they could find.

Torres knew he and his team would have to go through the multiple layers of rainforest tree cover to get on the ground. The overstory was the part of a tree jutting above the canopy—a dense ceiling of closely spaced branches. Below that was the understory, which had more widely spaced branches. The last layer was shrubs, the name sometimes confusing because, in the Amazon, these grew as high as twenty feet from the jungle floor. Because the trees in the area where the team was going had a species of kapok known as *Sumaumeira,* the highest in the Amazon, this made their descent through these layers even more perilous.

The Black Hawk arrived at the coordinates given to Torres and hovered ten feet above the overstory. As he expected, there was no sign of wreckage, the Javari Valley having swallowed the floatplane, adding it to the long list of secrets it kept. Each team member carried a rough terrain backpack weighing thirty-five pounds and an IMBEL 1A2 assault rifle with a silencer, both designed to operate in high-temperature jungle environments. On their waists, they wore a holstered Taurus PT-92 9 mm pistol with a seventeen-round magazine and a machete sheathed in a scabbard. Their camouflage uniform was waterproof and breathable, a necessity in the constant high temperature and humidity of the Amazon rainforest, which could get as much as four hundred inches of rain a year. Because this was the dry season, it only rained once a day. Therefore, everyone understood it was only a matter of time until the deluge came, which meant they needed to get below the canopy before it started.

As they hovered over their ingress point, their first task was to set up their communications system. They began by attaching an antenna to the overstory of the tallest kapok tree so the satcom dish had a line of sight with an orbiting satellite. A two hundred fifty-foot cable connected to the bottom of the dish—long enough to extend to the jungle floor. Once attached to the control panel, they'd have voice and data communications and GPS access.

Harnessed to a steel cable, Torres' first sergeant, Bolade Santiago, was the first to rappel from the helicopter. He was a stout person in his mid-thirties, five feet eight inches in height, with hickory-colored skin and short salt and pepper hair. Once clear of the fuselage, he motioned for the crew chief to lower him to the thick branch several feet below. Straddling it, he gave a thumbs up to send the satellite dish and attached electrical cable from the second winch. With the pilot holding the aircraft rock-steady, he used an impact driver to put heavy bolts into the sturdy tree branch, affixing the dish to it. He'd wait to uncoil the cable until descending to the jungle floor.

Torres, the next to rappel, was carrying the control panel and set down on the branch to the right of Santiago. The remaining six members followed, rappelling onto branches on either side of them. In their backpacks, they carried wireless signal boosters, which in a daisy chain arrangement, interfaced with the control panel and maintained signal strength as they moved through the rainforest. Their only limitation was that they could only carry a finite number of boosters. Therefore, as they went deeper into the rainforest, they'd eventually lose navigation and communication. However, Torres was counting on finding the wreckage long before then.

Penetrating the thick tree canopy required equal measures of patience and ingenuity. Because of its denseness, it was impossible to fast-rope to the jungle floor. Therefore, the Sixteenth Jungle Infantry Brigade employed a technique pioneered by the British SAS.

In the past, the standard method for getting troops to a remote area of forest or jungle was to have them parachute into the area and, when their parachute got ensnared in a tree, as it invariably did, descend to the ground by going from branch to branch. However, because some branches were far from the jungle floor, and it was easy to lose one's grip, these insertions were often perilous.

The SAS employed the technique of having each team member carry two hundred feet of rope, which they'd tie to the branch of whatever tree their parachute became entangled, and lower themselves to the forest floor. Since the canopy of a jungle is substantially denser than a forest, the Sixteenth modified the SAS system by rappelling onto the overstory, securing their rope, and using a carabiner, lowering themselves from branch to branch until clear to rappel to the ground. Torres' team were experts at this and set foot on the jungle floor an hour after Santiago left the helicopter.

On average, less than two percent of sunlight reaches the ground of most rainforests, where the air is hot, humid, and punctuated with a mustiness, similar to a greenhouse, that comes from the surrounding flora and trees, as well as decaying vegetation, wood, and flowers.

In contrast to what most might think, the jungle isn't quiet because it's teeming with life. The animals and insects combine to produce a constant background of humming, thrumming, buzzing, chirping, and other sounds. The loudest acknowledgment of one's existence came from the black howler monkey, which had a lion-like roar approaching one hundred forty decibels.

After Torres tested his headset mic with that of his men, he divided the squad into two-person teams. He made it clear that if one of them found the wreckage, they were to photograph the bodies, because there would be no survivors, and send the GPS coordinates to the rest of the team.

Two hours into their search, they discovered the wreckage half a mile from the coordinates Vilar gave Rocha. When Torres arrived, he looked towards the top of a giant kapok tree and saw the aircraft's wings. On the ground below it was a fuselage section with two passenger seats. There was no sign of the cockpit. Looking closely, he saw the unfastened seat belts. This meant the passengers they were after survived.

"How did they walk away from this?" Torres asked Santiago, who was to his right.

"Their luck will run out once we find them."

"Get Kito," he said, referring to Third Sergeant Kito Silva. The unit's tracker grew up in a small village in the Amazon Basin, where he learned his skills hunting small game to put food on his family's table.

While he waited, Torres called his commander, informing him they were still searching for the wreckage because it was not at the coordinates provided and that his squad would expand their search radius. His next call was to Rocha, giving him an accurate picture of the situation and saying they were going after the pair as soon as his tracker found their trail. However, in doing that, they could go beyond the range of the boosters and lose their communication link.

"They couldn't have gotten far. Even if they're uninjured, which I doubt, they're unfamiliar with the rainforest," Rocha said. "After you kill them, you'll need to bring their bodies back to the wreckage and photograph them there."

Torres knew Rocha wouldn't want to hear the reality of the situation, which was the possibility that the pair died in the jungle, and they would never find their bodies. The rainforest was so large and some areas so dense his squad could walk past them without noticing—assuming a predator hadn't taken them into their tree lair to feed the family. However, instead of giving him this dose of reality, he acknowledged his orders and ended the call.

Santiago arrived with Silva a few seconds after Torres finished his call. The tracker was five feet seven inches tall, bald, had cocoa-brown skin, light brown eyes, and was a trim one hundred fifty pounds. Looking around the wreckage site, he discovered the direction the survivors went after finding several circular indentations in the ground made by Cray's cane and two sets of boot prints that weren't military. These impressions weren't apparent because the team had walked unrestrained throughout the wreckage area obliterating large portions of the tracks. However, Silva could piece together the surviving fragments and, looking at the ground, led the squad down his version of the yellow brick road and into a section of the jungle for which no map existed.

"Tell me about yourself," Cray said as they continued to follow the gradual slope of the jungle floor.

"Okay, but I expect your bio afterward."

He nodded in agreement.

"I'm twenty-eight, born and raised in New York City, my parents live near me in Tribecca, no brothers or sisters, I've never been married, and I'm currently a leper to the magazine that commissioned me to photograph the loggers because I didn't deliver the photos nor answer their calls because I'm stuck in this god-forsaken place."

"How did you get into photography?"

"My mother gave me a camera when I was young, and it became my obsession as I grew older. When I was getting my Master of Arts degree, I took photography courses on the side at the New York Film Academy. After graduation, I discovered the salary for an MA degree wouldn't pay the bills in New York City, so I sold my photos online and to art shops to supplement my income. I got lucky when *National Geographic* published the pictures I took in the Occoquan Bay National Wildlife Refuge outside DC. The rest is history. Once your pictures are in that magazine, everyone wants to hire you. Since then, I've taken photographs of people and places all over the world. The only requirement was that I deliver them on time."

"What's the one place you photographed where you could spend the rest of your life?"

"That's an interesting question. In the United States?" Sanders asked.

"Yes."

"Rockport, Maine."

"I know it well. I grew up in Boston, slightly less than two hundred miles away. Why aren't you living there?" he asked.

"It's hard to make a living in a lobstering town of seven thousand."

"You don't look like the type to give up on a dream," Cray said.

"I'll move if the person I marry shares that dream and wants to raise our children there. My marriage and family would be a higher priority."

"Somehow, I think you would convince your husband that Rockport is that place. Do you have your sights set on a Mister Right who might give you that dream?" Cray asked.

"No one, currently. Several have been Mister Right Now, but none of them is my lifelong partner. What's your story, other than graduating last in a jungle survival class?"

"I'm thirty-nine, born in Boston, and an only child. I graduated from Harvard in 2005 with degrees in economics and statistical analysis. That same year, I went into the Army. Not much to tell after that, except that I became a Ranger and worked as an intelligence officer until I became a bean counter in the White House."

"You went from the holy grail of blue blood education to the Army? Explain," Sanders said.

"There was a war in Afghanistan, and I decided to serve my country rather than corporate America."

"What did your parents think of that?"

"It destroyed our relationship. My father was an investment banker and expected me to follow in his footsteps, but I wanted to serve my country."

"I could see where that might anger him, but why did that destroy your relationship?" she asked.

"My decision to join the Army became an embarrassment to my parents because of the social circles in which they moved. They believed that having a family member in the military was like saying your son was a blue-collar worker."

"Do you still talk with them?"

"Seldom. We mostly speak on holidays." Cray answered.

"When was the last time you saw them?"

"Several years ago. During that time, they didn't invite me to their house and declined invitations to mine. I took the hint."

"There has to be something more."

"Not if you know my parents. Mingling in the proper circles and becoming members of the right clubs means they're part of haute society. If I accompanied them to one of their clubs or functions, they would live in fear that someone would ask what I do and, upon finding out, question their societal status and not invite them to the right events. I know you can't understand that thinking, but some people are that way."

"Do you like what you do?" she asked, changing the subject.

"I can't imagine doing anything else. I made the right choice."

"Are you married? Do you have children, etcetera, etcetera?"

"I've never been engaged or married and don't have children."

"Any Ms. right now?"

"No. As you may have figured out, I'm not outgoing and am almost a recluse."

Sanders laughed.

"I don't go to bars, my friends are those I work with, and I spend most of my time reading intelligence reports. I'm not the type of person a woman looks for."

"Do you get lonely?"

"Sometimes. But I work through it."

"Sounds familiar."

"Bullshit. You're a gorgeous woman who can get a date at the drop of a hat, and you know it."

"I can always get a date with someone who takes me to dinner and thinks that entitles them to get into my pants that night or in the near future. I'm looking for something more than a romp in the sack or being with a person who wants me as a conquest and not someone with whom they want to grow old. Being beautiful doesn't always mean you get what you want. It makes it harder to find who's real and who's putting on a show."

"I never thought of that."

They continued talking. Five minutes later, they saw that the narrow path they were on ended at a wall of trees whose bases were so thick they nearly touched and, in between, was dense vegetation. Ten-foot-high shrub plants blocked their way to their left and right.

"We have to turn around. This is a dead end," Sanders said.

Cray inspected the shrubs on both sides of their path, seeing they were thick with long thorns. "We can't get through these without ripping our skin apart," he said. "Turning around also won't work because I didn't see another path on our way here. Our only option is to crawl through the thick vegetation between the trees. Because the jungle slopes that way, it's the direction we want to go. But, given your broken clavicle, crawling will be extremely painful."

"And we'll probably come face to face with something that wants to kill and eat us," Sanders added. "I'll put the weight on my good arm. If you don't go fast, I'll keep up."

"I'll keep it slow and sweep the area in front of me with the aluminum tube. Hopefully, that will scare away whatever's there."

"That's not a confidence builder."

Cray said he understood. Laying on his stomach and holding the cane in his left hand and the tubing in his right, he entered the dense growth. Because the light was dim, it was difficult to see with clarity more than a couple of feet in front of him. The vegetation they were crawling through was a mixture of sedges, a grasslike plant with triangular stems that grew in wet ground, and various ferns.

When he first entered the dense growth, he crawled using his knees and elbows, alternating pushing the cane and tube in front of him, hoping they would scare away snakes, tarantulas, and other deadly creatures. However, the first time he extended and returned the cane, it came back with a Brazilian wandering spider atop it. He immediately recognized the most venomous arachnid in the world, which had a body length of two inches and legs approaching seven inches. Its size, and the dark linear stripes on the appendages near its mouth, made it easy to identify. Cray may have been at the bottom of his jungle training class, but he had excellent recall for its deadly inhabitants from the Q cards he used in training. Gently lifting the cane, he flung the spider into the dense foliage to his left.

As he continued, he brushed aside two more Brazilian wandering spiders, a group of titan beetles that were six and a half inches long, several pink-toed tarantulas, and two snakes, which moved too fast for him to identify. Sixty yards later, with Sanders closely behind, they punched through the last of a tangled mass of ferns and found themselves in a small clearing. As they stood, both stared in wonderment at the twenty-foot waterfall before them. However, that amazement only lasted seconds before both began scratching.

"I almost forgot about jungle ants," Cray said. "In training, they got into my backpack, my fatigues, and even my weapon if I laid it down. We're lucky that we only encountered a few last night."

"They're irritating, but they don't sting."

"They're leaf-clutter ants and docile. The ones to worry about are bullet ants. They're an inch long, have large mandibles, and their sting inflicts serious pain. One bit me and it felt like someone poked a fiery blade into my body. The pain was excruciating and lasted several days."

They returned their attention to the waterfall.

"How is there a waterfall in the jungle?" Sanders asked.

"I heard there are quite a few, but this is the first I've seen."

Walking to the pool, they bent down and, parched from their crawl, took in large gulps of the clear water. As they stood, both again began scratching.

"We need to take a dip and get rid of these ants," Cray said.

"I won't argue with you."

Walking fully clothed into the cool water, he knew the ants wouldn't drown because they didn't have lungs. To waterproof themselves, they closed their spiracles, or holes on the sides of their bodies. Therefore, when he went into the water, they floated away. Sanders had the same experience.

The coolness of the water revived them. However, when Cray stepped out, his wound was throbbing. Unbuttoning his shirt, he saw his bandages had come off. The wound, which was red, puffy, and swollen, had a yellowish viscous fluid oozing from it.

Sanders saw this and put a hand to his forehead. "You have a temperature. We need to clean the wound, or it will get worse."

He squeezed his wound to see if more pus would come out. It did. "Who knows how many types of jungle bacteria entered my body through this hole," Cray said. Lifting his head and turning toward Sanders, he saw she'd taken off her clothes. Not unlike a deer transfixed by a vehicle's headlights, he stared at the statuesque blonde. "Your clavicle looks like it's healing," was all he could think to say.

"Thanks to you," she replied smiling, enjoying her companion's immobilization. "I'm going to wash my clothes, and you should do the same, or it'll worsen the infection."

He knew she was right and volunteered to wash their clothes since he had two good arms. When he finished, he hung them to dry over their improvised weapons. "In this humidity, I don't know if they'll dry," he said. "I'll build a fire to ensure they do. Since there's plenty of water here, and we'll have a fire, this is where we should spend the night."

Sanders agreed and, putting on her boots, volunteered to gather tinder.

An hour and a half later, they had dry clothes, after which they got dressed, and he returned her arm to a clean sling, the immobilization considerably lessening the pain she felt when it was off.

"Any idea where we're going to sleep?" Sanders asked. "The leaves around us are full of leaf-cutter ants."

"That's why I brought back these large branches and the bark I peeled from that young sapling," he said, pointing to his right. "I'm going to lash the branches together."

"And make what?"

"A raft or, more accurately, our bed."

"That's clever for an underachiever in survival training."

What they constructed was slightly over three feet wide and six feet long. Although they'd be floating in the water, Cray planned to anchor it to shore with a long braided strip of sapling bark so they could keep the fire roaring. That worked, and unlike the previous night, no predators ventured near them—either frightened by the fire or unable to get to their meal because of the water. Even though the raft was uncomfortable because the branches were rough and uneven, both slept soundly while holding one another to keep from rolling off the narrow slivers of wood and into the water.

"When's the last time you held someone all night?" she asked after she'd woken and saw Cray looking at her.

"It's been years. And you?"

"A little shorter. I enjoy being held."

They kept their embrace for a few more seconds before deciding it was time to get underway. Cray pulled them to shore.

"Do we continue following the jungle slope?" she asked as they began picking fruit to take with them.

"Yes, with a slight change. Do you see that stream of water leaving the pool?" he asked, referring to the thirty-six-inch wide rill that was less than a foot deep.

"We follow that?"

"It's flowing down to a larger body of water, which will be a tributary."

"Since this is the cleanest we're likely to look for a while, let me snap a few photos," she said, having difficulty removing the camera from her bag with one hand.

"Let me help," he said, removing the camera. After adjusting for the light, he took photos of the raft, the waterfall, and candid pictures of her. The last photo was a selfie of both smiling at the camera.

"How does the wound feel?"

"Sore, but I'll manage."

CHAPTER
FIVE

Torres' team lost communication and navigation when they went beyond the range of their last booster. Before losing contact, the captain called Rocha and told him that the two passengers in the floatplane had survived and were walking deeper into the Javari Valley.

"Do whatever it takes to ensure they don't make it out of there alive, and that no one will find their bodies," Rocha said. "The narrative has changed from dying in the crash to surviving but ill-advisedly walking into the jungle when they should have remained at the wreckage site. After an intense search by your squad, I'll say that you found no trace of them, and without food, water, or survival gear, they're presumed dead."

"I don't want to ruffle any feathers. My commander will need to let us continue a solo search and not send another team to assist."

"I'll handle it. I'll tell him I've ordered you to report your findings to me first."

"Candidly, this is as harsh a terrain as we've experienced. If they're not already dead, they soon will be. That's not fiction; it's a fact."

Rocha called Vilar, who called Bradford and told him of the new scenario. The FBI intel director said he didn't give a flip about how they died as long as Cray and the person with him met their end before they could speak with anyone. He reiterated the need for a photograph, with Vilar replying that, given the circumstances, providing that was a tossup.

"Silva," Torres called out after finishing his call.

The tracker came running from an area of dense vegetation.

"Where did they go? The cane and boot prints disappeared some time ago."

"That's because they're walking on plant leaves and debris. I've been following the subtler clues."

"Like what?"

"I noticed that the dry leaves on the ground, which are brittle, show a linear crack—indicating someone recently walked on them. I also saw that the wet leaves, with are naturally darker on the bottom, have their lighter side exposed. Given the lack of wind, someone brushed past them with their feet. But, to answer your question, they went into the vegetation between those two kapok trees," Silva said, pointing to it.

"Why there?"

Silva walked closer to the vegetation and pointed. "The leaves on rainforest vegetation are darker on the top and lighter on the bottom. The inverse is true here, meaning someone brushed against these plants."

"They're lost and should have turned around. Why are they going through this dense brush?"

"They're following the downward slope of the jungle floor, hoping that will lead them to a waterway, which it eventually will."

"That doesn't sound like the actions of someone unfamiliar with the jungle."

Silva agreed.

"How long until we catch them?"

"Someone disturbed these plants yesterday. Since we'll have a significantly faster pace, and if we don't lose their trail, we should catch them by late tomorrow or the following morning."

"You don't have your usual look of confidence."

"The Javari Valley makes me nervous."

That surprised Torres, who believed that Silva would track Satan through hell if asked.

"I grew up not far from this valley. I knew several people who thought they would sneak into it and come back with gold and other riches rumored to exist here. Instead, not one returned."

"There's a difference between someone from your village and this squad. When we put boots on the ground in the Javari Valley, we became the dominant force. We have enough firepower to handle any situation, and we'll wipe out any tribe or indigenous standing in our way."

He was wrong on both counts.

Following the stream was harder than Cray and Sanders imagined because they weren't walking on a trail but in a narrow, uneven water-filled trench carved into the rainforest floor. Infrequently, when it went through open spaces, they could get out of the trench and parallel it. However, most of the time, the denseness of the vegetation made that impossible, and they had to walk or crawl through the water. This sometimes proved dangerous, given they saw several golden dart frogs within arm's reach. A small amount of their venom, no more than three grains of table salt, was enough to kill a person. However, what concerned them the most were anacondas. They'd passed two sunning themselves beside the water, one ten feet in length and the other fifteen feet long.

Anacondas kill by constricting their prey and are non-aggressive unless defending themselves or deciding that it's time to eat. They can go for months without the dinner bell sounding. When it does, it can eat three hundred times its daily food requirement in one meal. Therefore, it's not unusual for them to consume something as large as a deer or human after crushing them with a force of nine thousand PSI.

Exhausted from two and a half days of walking and crawling with their injuries, once the stream emerged into a clearing, they crawled from the water and decided to stop for the day, build a fire, and dry their clothes. As their garments were drying, they gathered some of the low-hanging fruit around them and sat on a rock beside the fire, which they'd torched to get rid of ants and jungle organisms.

"I want you to do something for me, Erin," Cray said, both having transitioned to calling each other by their first name. "It won't be easy."

"So far, nothing we've done has been easy. What is it?"

"I want you to heat the end of my belt buckle and press it to my wound. It will never heal unless I cauterize it and kill the diseased tissue and bacterial infection causing this pus. It'll only worsen."

"As sick as you are, you can go into shock."

"I don't have a choice. I feel like I'm days away from dying if I can't get rid of this infection. If I die, you'll be by yourself and may not survive much beyond me. I have to live long enough to save you."

She kissed him, letting the kiss linger long enough to convey her feelings.

"I'm an idiot for not doing that to you first. I was too timid."

"I think we can safely eliminate timid from our vocabulary since we've seen each other naked," she replied.

He smiled briefly before again becoming serious. "When you press this to me," he said, removing his military-style belt, which had a rectangular buckle, and handing it to her, "keep it against the skin for several seconds."

"The pain will be intense."

"I'll bite down on this stick," he said, holding up a quarter-inch thick twig.

"When do you want to do it?"

"Now. The longer I wait, the more the infection will spread."

"Alright." With her arm free of the sling, she lowered the buckle over the fire and, once it was red-hot, dangled it next to the wound.

"Ready?

"Do it."

An instant later, she pressed it hard against his skin with the aluminum tube in her right hand.

Cray bit down hard on the twig and grunted, but sat motionless for the three seconds she pressed the buckle to the wound, with the smell of burning flesh temporarily overpowering the hothouse smell of the jungle. When she pulled it away, he collapsed to the ground on his back, with the twig still in his mouth and his eyes open. Putting her hand over his heart, she didn't feel a beat.

After pulling the twig from his mouth, she interlaced her fingers and began CPR, having learned it from a nurse who lived on the floor below her Tribeca loft, compressing his chest two inches at a pace of twice a second. Even though every compression caused her to scream in pain from the broken clavicle, she focused on squeezing the heart enough to pump blood cells, which contained oxygen, to critical organs like the brain. Twenty seconds later, he gasped for air, blinked, and looked up at his savior.

"That didn't go according to plan," he said in a low voice, making Sanders laugh.

Helping him sit against the rock, she took their homemade fruit container and filled it with water, half leaking out on the way to him. The water brought about a quick rebound.

"Nice job," he said, seeing the burnt skin in the shape of a belt buckle.

"Let's get you dressed, and during another one of delicious fruit dinners, you can explain how we survive another night in the jungle."

"I'd given that some thought. We start by gathering all the wood we can because we'll need every stick."

"What's the plan?"

He told her.

With Silva in the lead, followed in single file by Torres, Santiago, and the rest of the team, they hacked their way through the dense vegetation. The going was slow, the squad's tracker moving cautiously and stopping several times to scare away venomous snakes.

"Filho da puta," one of his men said as he slapped his neck. When he opened his hand, he saw that the one-inch long, eight-eyes arachnoid he'd flattened was a jumping spider, which wasn't harmful to humans. However, several steps later, the same person had the misfortune of brushing against a fern and got bit on the wrist by a wandering spider, which he reflexively crushed in the palm of his other hand. On seeing the spider's corpse on the ground, he immediately knew the seriousness of the situation and started hyperventilating. Hearing the commotion, Torres worked his way back to the bitten soldier, followed by Silva and Santiago.

"He has at most an hour," Silva whispered to Torres.

The captain nodded and, removing the pistol from its holster, put a bullet into the soldier's head. The rest of the squad, knowing that no one could save the soldier's life, understood the captain had made the right call. While they carried antivenoms in pre-filled syringes for various insect and snake bites, these didn't require refrigeration. The antidote for a wandering spider bite did, and that made it a no-go for jungle incursions.

"Divide his gear among the team," Torres told Santiago.

"We could cremate the body in the next clearing."

"That will slow us down, and the smoke from the fire will alert everyone in the area to our presence. I'm not going to lose anyone else."

Minutes later, the team hacked their way through the last of the dense vegetation and came to the waterfall.

"Why the raft?" Torres asked Silva when he saw it floating in the pool of water.

"They slept on it at night so the animals couldn't get to them."

"And they're still following the downward slope of the jungle floor?"

Silva pointed out the cane marks and footprints leading to the stream, which he said would eventually lead to a tributary.

"Can we catch them before nightfall?"

"Their imprints in the wet earth aren't well-defined, and the edges have eroded, showing they've dried during the day," Silva said. "That means they're six or seven hours ahead of us."

"Since we can't catch them before nightfall, we'll camp here for the night and end this chase tomorrow."

Silva didn't look convinced. Having lost one of the team, he was more convinced than ever that anyone entering the Javari Valley's uninvited wouldn't survive. His only question was whether it was the squad or those they were chasing who died first.

It took Sanders and Cray three hours to gather the quantity of firewood needed to last them through the night. They then carefully arranged the wood in a circle approximately ten yards in diameter. When they finished, they could barely stand.

The plan was to create a circle of fire around them, believing that animals and insects would instinctively avoid it. Knowing it would get hot in the middle of this circle and that they'd rapidly become dehydrated, Sanders used hollowed-out fruit, some of which were the size of a small watermelon, to store water.

As the jungle transitioned into darkness, Cray ignited the ring of wood. He told Sanders that the fire they built could only be robust enough to deter predators. Any larger and it would quickly consume their wood reserves and slow-cook them like a crock pot. An hour later, they got their first glimpse of a predator hunting for its next meal.

"Looks at those tusks," Cray remarked, pointing to a wild boar visible in the light cast by the fire. The four hundred pounds animal was three feet high at the shoulders, five feet three inches long, and had five-inch tusks.

"Are they carnivores?"

"Omnivores. They eat plants and animals."

"How would it fare against a jaguar?"

"We'll find out," he said, pointing to the lower branch of a tree on the other side of the stream. Unlike the jaguar which approached them the first night, this one was a third smaller, weighing two hundred pounds.

"It doesn't look like he's interested in the boar."

"The jaguar may be the dominant apex predator, but its instinct or experience is telling it those razor-sharp tusks would take a chunk out of it."

The boar, not seeing the jaguar and with no easy prey within sight, returned to the dense vegetation and disappeared. Seeing this, the jaguar shifted its focus to the two humans in the center of the fire. Deciding to stake out a position on the ground, it jumped down and waited beside the stream, far enough away from the fire to stay cool.

"What is it with jaguars and fire?" Sanders asked. "It doesn't seem to deter them for long."

"It's probably hungry and will wait us out, instinctively knowing this fire won't last forever."

"I'll get my camera and see if the flash will scare it away." When she returned, she saw the jaguar was crossing the stream. As she snapped photo after photo with her flash, it stopped mid-steam but didn't run from the light flashes.

That's when it happened. Suddenly, a fifteen feet long green anaconda, one of the two seen earlier, sprang from the water and bit the animal behind the neck, its backward curving inner teeth grabbing the predator while its body wrapped around it. Heavier than its prey by a hundred pounds, the snake tightened its grip, crushing the jaguar as it pulled it into the stream. In less than a minute, its jaws detached, and it slowly began swallowing its prey.

"I'm glad he wasn't hungry when we saw it," Sanders said.

"Snakes are cold-blooded. During the day, they soak up the warmth and are half asleep unless disturbed. They mostly hunt at night. If we didn't have this fire, that could have been one of us."

She began to shake, and he put his arms around her.

They slept in shifts, each getting four hours of sleep before the dimness of daylight penetrated the canopy. Sanders' broken clavicle had swollen considerably from the previous day because of the CPR. Although in a lot of pain, she didn't tell Cray because he had problems of his own, and she didn't want him to worry about her.

"Let me look at that wound again," she said when they awoke. Inspecting it, she found that, although there was no pus, there were now red streaks around the spot she'd cauterized. He was also running a high fever.

"How do you feel?"

"Like hell, but we need to keep moving."

"Those red streaks don't look good."

"It's nothing," he replied.

After gathering fruit, they broke camp and continued following the stream.

Torres' team had a different approach to staying alive at night. To protect themselves from predators, they killed every creature they saw. With their night vision goggles and advanced weaponry, gunfire echoed throughout the jungle, and by daylight, an enormous number of carcasses littered the camp's perimeter.

CHAPTER
SIX

The person who directed Bradford to kill Cray was a shadowy person known as the thin man, a reference to his rail-thin appearance. His given name was Harrison Carter, although he sometimes used Tenant Masterson as an alias. The fifty-eight years old British citizen weighed one hundred thirty pounds soaking wet, was six feet three inches tall, had a pale complication, pinched nose, blue eyes, and crooked teeth that were always yellowed because he rarely went to a dentist. For generations, his family made money trafficking Afghanistan opium. After being laundered, he used it to buy legitimate businesses through shell corporations and to form a private fund. These made him one of the twenty wealthiest persons in the world, although he was the only one who knew.

Through the years, he formed relationships with those who aligned with his personal and business philosophies. This cadre of like-minded individuals quickly expanded to include politicians, government officials, those in national and local law enforcement, and numerous billionaires. They met annually at Carter's mansion in Davos, Switzerland, formalizing their relationship into an organization called the Cabal and selecting the thin man as their leader.

Their goal was to create a new world order—an authoritarian one-world government where a single, borderless society replaced nation-states. One might ask why Carter and other billionaire Cabal members, who could purchase whatever they desired, and those of influence who were on a gravy train for life, wanted to risk it all for this NWO. The reason was they expected even greater wealth and power—an aphrodisiac to every member who knew that creating a singular society resulted in monopolistic control over every industry, service, and other facet of daily life for nearly eight billion people. The Kool-Aid they'd hand to the masses in assembling this control was the panacea that a single global leadership would eliminate wars, poverty, and every other ailment of society. This panacea wasn't a hard sell since everyone wanted a better, easier life, and no one trusted career politicians, whose idea of the common good ended with themselves; the government, whose policies changed with the political agenda of those elected to office; or a dictatorship assuming power.

The Cabal poured billions of dollars into national and local governments to elect individuals who believed in a new world order and hired lobbyists, union members, and other influencers to plant the seeds of their reformation globally. With public relations firms pushing the advantages of an NWO—politicians, corporations, and the populace became increasingly enamored with the idea of a one-government society that offered cradle-to-grave care for every human while eliminating societal ill. These ideas gained traction when governments around the world could not make life better for their citizenry while those elected to office feathered their beds. Over time, the combination of the Cabal's PR efforts and the government's inability to make life better resulted in uniting the planet behind a singular focus—a new world order that promised a better life.

The media—whose mantra was ready, fire, aim, were behind this singular society because they'd long advocated egalitarianism. Their colleagues ostracized or fired anyone with a contrarian viewpoint and banned them from social media for not going off the cliff with the other lemmings. With social, print, and digital media encouraging the radical change to a new world order, they considered those who offered dissent to be irrational. Dissenters were subsequently told by the lemmings they were too ignorant to make an informed decision, even though anyone who received higher than a D- in economics, supply chain management, or business administration knew that a lack of competition and checks and balances on overseers worked against the common good.

The first significant bump in the road for the Cabal occurred when they learned Cray suspected an organization like theirs existed. However, because he knew the Marine intelligence officer didn't have a shred of proof, Carter ignored him. His attitude quickly changed when he discovered Cray was coming to Davos, Switzerland, to attend the World Economic Forum. Fearing this was a guise and that he knew more than believed about their organization and would destroy decades of work, Carter hired an ex-SAS assassin to kill him. However, the assassin only wounded him, and before becoming unconscious, Cray whispered the word "cabal" to Matt Moretti. The thirty-nine-year-old ex-Army Ranger was six feet three inches tall, had a chisel-cut face, thick-chested muscular physique, and close-cut black hair in which gray had yet to intrude. He was the warrior who led Nemesis in the field.

Once the black ops group became involved and found Cray's notes, the team went to Davos to investigate the Cabal. From the moment they arrived, they were in a battle for their lives before ending the confrontation by sending a howitzer shell into the snowy mountain peak above Carter's mansion. The ensuing avalanche killed hundreds of Cabal members, including most of the leadership. However, the thin man survived and escaped to his off-the-grid private island residence in the Maldives, located six hundred and ten miles from the coast of Sri Lanka. From there, he communicated through Tor with Bradford, one of the few senior Cabal members who didn't go to Davos.

Nemesis comprised eleven people. Five were operatives, two techs, and an administrative head, who was Cray. Headquarters was at the Raven Rock Mountain Complex offices, referred to as Site R. The six hundred fifty acres underground facility near the

Pennsylvania/Maryland border was a backup to the Pentagon and connected to Camp David by a six-and-a-half mile tunnel. The president authorized space at the complex for his White House Statistical Analysis Division, which was the team's cover, allowing them to work there and speak with him without creating suspicion because their job description was that they were presidential bean counters. Two team members, Adam Daller and Pete Sherman provided drone support from Creech Air Force Base in Nevada. The last member of the team was General Chien An of the PLA. Living in Beijing, he was the Chinese government's liaison providing intel and support.

With Cray's departure from Washington Dulles International Airport to Manaus five days ago, those at Nemesis began working to discover where Harrison Carter and the other Cabal members who didn't die in the avalanche were hiding. Because they wanted Cray to have a well-deserved rest, and the crash never made the papers, those at Nemesis assumed he was having a good time and keeping his workaholic instincts in check by not calling. However, none thought that would last for the entire thirty days he was on leave.

To ferret out the surviving Cabal members, Moretti enlisted the help of Libby Parra—Chief of the Global Issues Analysis Office at NSA headquarters at Fort Meade, Maryland. She and Moretti had previously worked together, and she was one of a few outsiders who knew about the ultra-secret organization. Parra was a forty-eight-year-old statuesque blonde who'd kept her beauty as she aged. Never wanting to get married, although she'd had several proposals, she'd worked at the Agency for thirty years and told her boss she was going to continue until dropping at her desk.

The information that Moretti wanted was at the NSA's Utah Data Center near Bluffdale. This facility was the Agency's all-inclusive library which stored every byte of communication, data, and personal information collected by its satellites, marine, ground, and airborne systems. This included American citizens' private emails, cell phone calls, internet searches, and personal data trails, including parking receipts, travel itineraries, bookstore purchases, and other digital information that the Agency referred to internally as pocket litter.

One reason the Cabal escaped detection for so long was that its members communicated through an NSA satellite using set-aside frequencies. These, along with a protocol to access the satellite, gave a select few the ability to bypass the NSA's voice and data algorithms. The Agency did this for reasons of internal security so that these designated few could candidly communicate without fear that someone like Edward Snowden could access and disseminate their conversations or data. It didn't mean they didn't intercept the transmissions, because the NSA recorded everything. It only meant they wouldn't scrub the intercept through the Agency's algorithms, which flagged anything that analysts should look closely at. Parra had previously discovered the Cabal's use of the satellite, but not who'd compromised the system. Therefore, she didn't know that Samuel Bradford gave this information to Carter, who distributed it to the other Cabal members.

Bradford and the rest of the Cabal assumed they weren't being intercepted and recorded because the frequencies bypassed the analytical process. Wrong. He also believed that his Tor conversations were private, which was also incorrect. Therefore, once Parra found out they were using the NSA's satellite, she retrieved those recordings. She also recovered his Tor conversations and the recordings of Vilar, Rocha, and Torres, forwarding them to the techies at Nemesis—Kyle Alexson and Mike Connelly. Both were Ph.D. grads from MIT who formerly worked at the NSA. From this information, they compiled a list of Cabal members and those with whom they associated.

"Although most are dead, they were a much larger organization than I assumed," Han Li said to her husband. The thirty-six-year-old, five-foot eleven-inch tall statuesque beauty had long brunette hair, an athletic build, and a voice like Angelina Jolie. Formerly

China's premier assassin, she was married to Moretti. Both were sitting at the conference room table with the rest of the team, each looking at their iPads and the enormous amount of data assembled by the techies.

"Samuel Bradford, the FBI's intel director, and Desmond Pruitt at the Department of Transportation are the only surviving Cabal members within the United States government now that the Attorney General fired the FBI director," Jack Bonaquist said. The former Secret Service agent was thirty-five years old, six feet eight inches tall, weighed two hundred forty pounds, and had a face reflecting his square-jawed sternness of not mincing words.

"The president should get rid of Bradford and Pruitt," Blaine McGough said. The twenty-eight year old former Force Recon Marine was six feet two inches tall and three hundred five pounds of solid muscle.

"We discussed that," Moretti responded. "He feels that one or both are still communicating with Carter, although not over an NSA satellite since they changed protocols. He doesn't want to fire them yet if they can lead us to him. The other problem is that by law, the NSA can only monitor an American's international phone calls if they're speaking with a foreigner who is a surveillance target."

"You and I both understand that's not true," Bonaquist countered, "because of a large loophole in the law that permits them to presume their prospective surveillance targets are foreigners outside the United States absent specific information to the contrary. That presumption makes anyone fair game for warrantless surveillance."

"I know, Jack, but the president doesn't want to make that loophole the headline on the nightly news. As far as Nemesis is concerned, if Bradford or Pruitt were involved with the attempts on Cray's life, we're going to make sure they will not try and get immunity for their testimony, take the fifth, or appear in court. Their next appearance will be in the morgue."

"Problem solved," Bonaquist replied.

CHAPTER
SEVEN

"How are you doing?" Sanders asked Cray, seeing that he was becoming increasingly fatigued and more dependent on his cane.

"I've got a headache, I'm tired, and my wound hurts like a bitch," he responded in a weary voice.

"Do you want to take a breather?"

"I learned in the Army that if you keep putting one foot in front of the other, you eventually get to where you're going no matter how unpleasant the journey. How's the clavicle?"

"It hurts like a bitch," she said, repeating what Cray said about his wound and making him laugh. "It feels like someone is jabbing a thick needle into it with every step I take. We're quite the pair. At least the area on both sides of this stream is clear, and we don't need to crawl through the water. When I recall the anaconda eating that jaguar, I shiver thinking about us crawling through that water and seeing that very snake."

"Very few creatures in this rainforest don't want to kill us to protect themselves or make you and me part of their diet. Tell me when you're thirsty, and I'll cut open another vine."

"Now would be a good time," she said, noticing that he was panting. "We don't have to push ourselves; we can make camp whenever we want and put one foot in front of the other tomorrow."

Cray cut open two vines, and they drank the clear liquid. When they finished, he looked for ants before sitting on the ground. Sanders followed.

"I don't think I have another day in me, Erin. My forehead feels significantly warmer than this morning, meaning the infection in my body is spreading. We need to walk as far as we can today to get you close to the tributary or other body of water into which this stream flows. If there's anyone in the area, they'll be on it."

"To get us closer, not me," she corrected. "I'm not leaving you. We're a team."

"I don't want to leave you either. But without antibiotics, I'm going to die. That's a given. I'm okay with my death, but not yours. I have to get you in a position where you'll survive when I'm gone. That's why we need to keep going until we reach the water. Once you're there, you'll make it because, as a New Yorker, you've handled adversity all your life."

That remark brought a laugh.

"I wish I'd known you sooner, Erin."

She didn't speak. Instead, she kissed him gently on the lips and took his hand.

"Let's see what's in store for us," he said, getting up and throwing his aluminum tube to the ground.

She did the same, correctly sensing that he'd gotten rid of his weapon to take her hand.

As Cray and Sanders left, a pair of eyes watched their every move from the dense brush. The tribesman stood five feet three inches tall, was in his late teens, had piercing brown eyes, bronze-toned skin, and tattoos on both cheeks that imitated the whiskers of a jaguar. His hair was black and styled in what westerners would call a buster boy haircut. On his face were streaks of red paint, which he and other members of his tribe applied to themselves daily—the design depending on their mood that day. This warrior's design was a thick line below each eye and across the top of his forehead.

The tribesman was naked except for a loincloth. Tied to holes in it by leather strings were a blowgun and a pouch of poison darts. On the thick black leather rope around his waist were his most prized possessions—the shrunken heads of four former enemies whose souls he now controlled because it was well-known to the people of his tribe that a person's spirit lived in their head.

The headhunter's name within his tribe was Shining Anaconda—the only surviving son of Proud Bird, the leader of the Shuars. The young warrior was taking one of the village canoes to the village fishing area, where he'd use a handmade net to catch peacock bass, pacu, silver dollar, and armored catfish—which coexisted alongside the red-belly piranhas which infested the waters. Since his village was upstream, it took some effort to go against the current of the Amazon tributary and get to the fishing area. However, the effort was always worth it because not only was the net fishing good, but the game was more abundant and easier to kill in this area.

This morning, there was the smell of burnt wood drifting over the water. Because this slice of jungle belonged to his tribe, he investigated the source of the smoke. Pulling his canoe ashore, he let his sense of smell guide him, unslinging the bow from his shoulder and taking an arrow from his weathered leather quiver as he walked. The smell of smoke got stronger the further he went inland. However, this didn't have the denseness of a jungle fire, which he'd experienced when lightning ignited a kapok tree near his village. That blaze quickly spread to surrounding trees creating two hundred feet high torches that became extinguished only when heavy rains pummeled the area.

As he followed the smell, he heard footsteps coming in his direction. Moments after hiding in the dense vegetation, he saw white people, the first he'd ever seen, passing within inches of him. His initial instinct was to kill them with a poison-tipped arrow or dart from his blowgun so that he could add their heads, called tsantsas within his tribe, to his collection. These unique trophies were sure to give him added prestige in his village. However, he felt such an action might displease his father, who wouldn't share in his son's good fortune by him beheading the trespassers and adding their heads to his collection. Therefore, he would capture and take the intruders to his village to be displayed and give his father the choice of which person he wanted to behead.

Torres' squad, minus one, significantly increased their pace as they followed the stream. Since they had machetes, there was no need to crawl through the sections of it where vegetation enshrouded both sides. Instead, they cautiously hacked their way through the jungle, scaring or brushing away numerous snakes, spiders, and other venomous rainforest inhabitants. Three hours after they broke camp, they entered the clearing where Cray and Sanders spent the night.

"Why won't they die?" Torres asked, the irritation clear in his voice as he kicked one of the charred pieces of wood that showed how they were able to survive the night. "Which way did they go?" he asked Silva.

"They're still following this stream," he said, having knelt to look at the ground closer. "These indentations are deeper and are more closely spaced than before, showing they're tired."

"So are we. Let's get this over with. Move out."

Shining Anaconda silently paralleled Cray and Sanders, racing ahead to position himself at a bend in the path twenty yards ahead of them. Sanders, who was the first to see him, screamed when she saw the tribesman and the band of trophies around his waist. Cray focused on the arrow nocked in his bow and pointed at him. They stood motionless as he approached.

"He's a headhunter," Sanders said.

"I know. I'm guessing he'd like nothing better than adding us to his collection. Do you see that black tar-like substance on the tip of the arrow? I think it's poison. All the arrow has to do is nick us, and we're dead. If I can get close enough, I can strip him of that bow and render him unconscious with a headlock."

"He's half your age, and his tribe is probably nearby. We might run into more of them."

"You're right. It doesn't look good, but it's all we've got. Let's see if he gives me an opening," Cray said.

The tribesman began yelling at them in his language. Although they didn't understand, they figured out he was telling them to shut up. Once they did, he motioned with his bow for them to continue following the stream. An hour later, they entered a small clearing behind which was a tributary of the Amazon—a tributary being a freshwater stream that flows into a larger stream or river. On the bank was a dugout canoe carved from a hollowed tree, with a fishing net and crude paddle inside. After motioning for his captives to sit, Shining Anaconda dragged the heavy canoe to the water's edge. Returning to where Cray and Sanders were sitting, he nodded towards the canoe, signaling them to get in. Cray didn't move and told Sanders to keep still, believing that they were as good as dead once they were in the canoe.

Knowing that the native's tribe wasn't in the area, or he wouldn't be using a canoe, Cray wanted the tribesman to come a couple of steps nearer so that he'd be close enough to grab and pull him to the ground. With the couple not cooperating, just as the tribesman took that second step to force them to their feet, the uncertain hand of fate intervened when Torres' squad emerged from the jungle. When they did, all eyes riveted on them.

"Kill him; they're about to escape," Torres said, pointing to Cray when he saw him and Sanders sitting near a canoe with a tribesman motioning for them to get in.

Cray and Sanders didn't understand Portuguese. Therefore, seeing the Brazilian soldiers, they believed this was a rescue party that had somehow followed them through the rainforest. That belief evaporated when bullets started flying at Cray, missing him only because he laid flat when he saw the soldiers turning their weapons toward him. Sanders hit the ground a split second later.

"They're trying to kill me," Cray said, noticing that the tribesman came to the same conclusion and distanced himself from them. Crawling to where he was standing, Cray grabbed his legs and pulled him to the ground as a burst of bullets ripped past the two and shredded the plants' several yards behind them.

From the confused expression on his face, the tribesman believed Cray had saved his life. He gestured for Sanders and Cray to follow him into a barely discernable opening in the vegetation alongside the water.

"What do you think?" Sanders asked.

"Do we have a choice? We'll be an easy target if we stay in the open."

They both followed the tribesman.

"After them," Torres ordered. As he ran, he focused on where he saw them enter the vegetation. However, when he got there, there were several openings, all going in slightly different directions. Only when Silva joined him several seconds later did he know which space they entered.

The chase began with Torres believing that, with Silva's tracking skills and the squad's firepower, the three were only prolonging the inevitable. This conclusion seemed solid when Silva found Cray's cane in the dense vegetation alongside what he would describe as a snake path through the undergrowth, confirming to the captain that someone had roughly brushed the plants along the path. Hearing this, Torres bolted ahead, believing the three were only a stone's throw away. The rest of the squad quickly followed. The balloon burst one hundred fifty yards later when he and the rest of the squad reached a wall of trees surrounded by dense vegetation.

"Where are they?" Torres asked Silva, the tone of his voice questioning his tracking skills.

Silva didn't want to tell him they were in this mess because he'd taken off down this path before he could analyze whether they tricked them into following a false trail. Because the captain and the rest of the team trampled the narrow ground and brushed the surrounding vegetation, he couldn't see whether there was a lack of clues that showed they didn't come this way.

"There are no footprints in this soft ground, and the vegetation ahead is undisturbed," Silva told him. We followed a false trail. The only way to find them is to return to where we found the cane and examine the underbrush."

"Merda," Torres said, knowing he was at fault for leading the charge and not following his tracker. Taking a deep breath, he told Silva to lead the way.

Shining Anaconda, Cray, and Sanders lay catatonically still in the dense vegetation as Torres' squad took off in a direction ninety degrees from where they were hiding. The tribesman had earlier grabbed Cray's cane before returning without it a few seconds later and signaling for everyone to lay prone. Once the soldiers passed, he motioned for them to follow him as they circled back to the canoe. When they arrived, and without threatening them with an arrow, he pointed to the canoe.

"This defines being caught between a rock and a hard place," Cray said as he got into the canoe with Sanders following.

Once they got in, the tribesman pushed the dugout log until the water got beneath it and hopped in. Grabbing the paddle, he took long powerful strokes, quickly increasing their speed and distance from shore. Within minutes, the canoe rounded the bend and was out of sight.

Torres and his squad arrived at the spot where the canoe had been several minutes after it left shore.

"A canoe means the native's village will be close," Silva volunteered, although he instantly regretted saying it because he saw the person they were trying to catch was a headhunter, and the last thing he wanted was to find their village.

"Unless we have a boat, we'll need to parallel the bank to find where they came ashore. If they went to the other side of the water, we'll need to build a raft. Both will take too much time, and we'll lose them." Seeing there was sky and not a canopy of trees, he removed the satphone from his backpack. "I need to make a call."

Rocha was short on patience and long on anger when he heard Cray had reached the tributary and escaped.

Because of this, Torres waited before explaining about the dugout canoe and headhunter. He'd save that for their next conversation. "I need a river boat with firepower," Torres said.

"I'll have a Black Hawk airlift a LAR," the colonel answered, referring to a fast attack boat. "Give me your coordinates, and you'll have it tomorrow. This operation has been very messy, captain. The longer you're in the field, the more questions I'm asked. Put those two in the ground and ensure no one ever finds their bodies."

CHAPTER
EIGHT

"This isn't good," Moretti said as he looked at his iPad, the team viewing Bradford, Vilar, Rocha, and Torres' intercepts sent by Libby Parra.

"Put those two in the ground and ensure no one ever finds their bodies," Moretti read. "The Brazilian military is intent on killing Cray and whoever is with him. With their resources, it's only a matter of time until they succeed."

"Can you give me a visual of the coordinates for the boat drop so we can look at the area?" Han Li asked Connelly, who was sitting at the end of the conference room table with his laptop in front of him.

Accessing a government database, he projected a map onto the giant LED screen at the head of the table. A red pin showed the location.

"Where does that river flow?" Han Li asked.

Connelly widened the view, showing it flowed into the Amazon River.

"With the firepower on that LAR, they'll be dead before long," Bonaquist said.

"Not if we act fast enough," Moretti replied. Knowing the president was at Camp David, he called and asked for a meeting.

Moretti's call wasn't unusual. With the president establishing Nemesis to avoid bureaucratic paralysis by analysis, where even the slightest delay in solving a strategic problem could critically harm the nation, his conversations with Cray and Moretti were typically spur-of-the-moment. Therefore, he told him he'd have a cup of coffee waiting.

Moretti used the tunnel to get to Camp David and was there in ten minutes. After clearing security, he parked in an adjacent parking area where a Secret Service agent was waiting beside a golf cart and drove him to the presidential cabin, Aspen Lodge. When he entered the living room, he found POTUS sitting in his favorite leather club chair with a coffee cup. The president motioned to take the chair to his left.

"I told the kitchen you like the Nespresso's Stormio coffee," Ballinger said, pointing to a white mug with the presidential seal on the side table

"You have an excellent memory, sir."

"Since time is always of the essence when you request a meeting, what's going on?"

Moretti detailed the NSA's communication intercepts, beginning with Bradford ordering Cray's plane to be destroyed over the Amazon rainforest. When he finished his briefing twenty minutes later, he handed the president a printed copy of the intercepts that Alexson gave him before he left.

The president was visibly angry, his voice displaying his outrage. "Is there some reason I shouldn't have Bradford and Pruitt perp-walked out of their government offices and thrown in jail?"

"If you arrest them, it'll be significantly more challenging finding Carter, and the communications between Vilar, Rocha, and Torres might end. If that happens, finding Cray will be next to impossible because we only know his approximate location because Torres is chasing him.

"What are your plans after you find Cray and the person with him?"

"I don't plan to balance the scales of justice in a courtroom. I plan to kill every person involved with the Cabal, not only because they killed a member of my team and made numerous attempts on our lives, but because they're a threat to this nation."

"Make that happen," the president said in a resolute voice. "How long can Cray and whoever he's with survive once this boat arrives?"

"Not long. It's a game changer. However, according to the conversation between Rocha and Torres, it won't come until tomorrow."

"What's your plan to insert your team without being discovered and find and save them when you don't know their exact location?" Moretti told him.

"If your plan doesn't work, Cray won't be the only one Torres is chasing."

Moretti said that he didn't have a choice given the time constraints. "Because our timeline is critical, I'll need a lot of gear and a transport aircraft within the hour."

"I'll handle it."

"Your flight is twelve hours long?"

"Thirteen," Moretti corrected.

"Thirteen," the president repeated. "You need to get moving. What if Torres' boat arrives early and they leave before you get there?"

The NSA is monitoring his conversations. But we're out of luck if he doesn't give Rocha a new set of coordinates."

"I wish I could move an NSA or CIA satellite over the area, but if I do, the intel community will want to know why, and which black ops group I'm supporting. Those questions are unanswerable. Also, I can't emphasize enough that your insertion must be innocuous because the United States doesn't have a military presence in Brazil. Their president is adamant that he wants to eliminate all foreign military on their soil and rebuild their military so that Brazilians will never need to ask a foreign government for protection. He won't let me put boots on the ground in his country."

"I can't say that I disagree with their philosophy of being self-reliant."

"Me either. Therefore, if the Brazilians discover your team, their president will sever diplomatic relations with the United States to make him look strong to his people and the rest of Latin America. If that happens—Congress, the DOD, and the justice department will investigate my actions."

"We might start a shit storm, but no one will know who we are, and we'll bring Cray and whoever he's with back safely."

"Give me a list of the gear you need, and I'll order the commander of Joint Base Andrews to pull those assets from the armory."

Moretti wrote out the list.

"I'll tell him I classified your mission as top secret, special compartmented information—presidential eyes only. That means everyone involved will keep what they hear and see to themselves. When's the last time you were in the jungle?"

"In 2007. Cray and I were in the same class at Ranger school and went to jungle survival training together. After we graduated, the Army needed bodies in Afghanistan and sent us there."

"How did you do in the jungle?"

"Number one in my class."

"And Cray?"

"Aced the knowledge portion of the course, but his body couldn't handle the ninety-two-degree heat and ninety percent humidity. He became prematurely fatigued—significantly more than anyone else in the class. Doug wasn't a quitter. He worked as hard as the rest of us, but his kryptonite was high heat and high humidity. However, he was fine with the lower sixty percent humidity of the Middle East."

"How did he pass the course?"

"In the military, you're a team. If someone falls behind and needs help, one person gets under one arm, another under the other, and we make sure we all get to where we're going together, so we're technically graded equally. Since we finished maneuvers as a team, and he was at the top of our class with the knowledge portion, he passed. However, the instructors' attached their evaluations and comments to each of our performance reports. The brass wanted to keep Doug in the Rangers, so they put him in an office, not in the field."

"He's back in the jungle, but this time he's recovering from a gunshot wound and being chased by professional soldiers. How long will he last?"

"We need to find him as soon as possible."

When Moretti returned to Site R, he found the team still sitting at the conference room table and looking at their iPads. They looked up as he approached.

"It's a go," he stated. Expecting an enthusiastic response, since it meant they got the go-ahead to rescue Cray, the lack of elation surprised him. "What did I miss?" he asked.

"Libby sent us more translated intercepts. Torres told Rocha that Cray and the woman with him encountered a headhunter who took them away in his canoe," Han Li answered.

"A headhunter?"

"That's what Torres said."

"They may already be dead," Bonaquist added.

"Absent evidence to the contrary, we'll assume they're alive," Moretti replied. "If Torres' squad remains as good as they have been tracking them, they'll find where the canoe came ashore and follow the headhunter wherever they're going. We find Cray by following Torres' squad."

"How?" McGough asked.

"Since the boat isn't coming until tomorrow, we get there in time to follow it. The president is giving us transport to Brazil; all the gear we need will be on it."

"What boat did you tell him we wanted?" McGough asked.

Moretti told him.

"That's a good choice. It's quiet, and we can follow the LAR with no one hearing us."

"I get the insertion, but how do we exfil with Cray and the woman?" Bonaquist asked.

Moretti told him.

"I'm sorry I asked."

"Change into jungle fatigues and grab your weapons," Moretti said. "Our transport is on the helipad, and we're wheels up when we get to Joint Base Andrews."

CHAPTER

NINE

An hour after their escape, the tribesman steered the canoe to shore three miles downstream and on the opposite bank from where they entered the water, dragging the heavy canoe behind dense brush where it would be impossible to see. Returning to the water's edge, he grabbed a flat stone and, getting down on his knees, smoothed away the drag marks and footsteps visible in the mud. Once he finished, Shining Anaconda motioned for Cray and Sanders to follow, leading them into the jungle through a nearly invisible slit in the dense vegetation. As he walked, the native beat the ground in front and the vegetation beside him with a practiced rhythm to frighten or brush away any creature that might bite or fasten itself to them.

With Cray deteriorating rapidly, the going was slow. His infection was spreading, and in defense of the body, his immune system was releasing inflammatory chemicals that increased the core temperature to try and "cook" the invading virus. With a fever of near one hundred four degrees, the body's all-out attack on the virus caused him a throbbing headache and made it difficult to breathe in the high humidity. Sanders, seeing him struggle, moved in front of him and, putting his arms over her shoulders, absorbed the piercing pain from her clavicle as she followed the tribesman through the slit of vegetation.

Half a mile later, they entered the headhunter village. In the center of the clearing was a shabono—the single-roof living quarters for the tribe of sixty people. The hundred yards long, oval-shaped thatched structure looked generations old and frequently patched since then.

Walking through one of the four thatch doors leading into the structure, all eyes turned to the foreigners, who were without restraints or threatened with a weapon. No one in the village had ever seen a Caucasian, and when Sanders lowered Cray to the ground, the curious approached and began poking them with their fingers to ensure they were real and not spirits.

Proud Bird, the tribe's leader, and Shining Anaconda's father, lifted himself off his mat and approached his son. He wore no symbol to show his position of authority because it was unnecessary. Everyone respected him as their leader and understood that by custom, his son would replace him upon his death. There was no anger in the old man's eyes, only curiosity as to why the two before him were alive and hadn't had their heads lopped off by his son since they were valuable trophies worthy of display.

Greeting between family members and those within the tribe was verbal, and there was no shaking of hands, hugs, or other forms of physical contact. Communication was straightforward. If they had something to say, they got straight to the point; if not, they remained silent.

"Are these your prisoners?" Proud Bird asked.

"I captured them within our tribal area, but the man saved my life."

His father now understood why Shining Anaconda hadn't killed the intruders. Tribal custom dictated that being saved from death indebted that person to their savior until they performed an equal act of heroism or that person released them from their obligation. His son had no choice but to spare the intruders and bring them to the village to protect them.

Turning to his tribe, he acknowledged his son's obligation and said the intruders were their guests and were to be cared for and protected. Everyone accepted this without question.

With Cray unconscious and lying on his back, Sanders looked around the shabono, noticing that most of the men had shrunken heads tied around their waist, certain that she and Cray would adorn someone's body before long. However, her concern evaporated when several of the tribe's women pushed their mats close together, creating space for the two additional mats that one brought. She saw each tribe member had their living space, designated by woven mats, which served as a sleeping, eating, and social area.

At Proud Bird's direction, several men carried Cray to one and gently laid him flat, while the women led Sanders to the other and gave her food and drink. Seeing that Cray was in terrible straits, an older woman placed her hand on his forehead and, with a look of concern, stripped off his clothing. Her attention immediately focused on the wound and the pus emerging from it.

She spoke rapidly to four women near her, who left and returned a few minutes later with dried plants, a stone bowl, and a hollowed gourd containing water. Working as a team, they crushed the plants and poured a precise amount of water into the bowl, mixing it into a brown paste. The older woman applied it to Cray's wound and covered that with the fungus that another woman had retrieved from the jungle. Once the microorganisms in the fungus came in contact with the paste, another woman dipped a wooden dart in the paste residue at the bottom of the stone bowl and poked Cray's torso. She repeated the process, each time drawing blood as she drove the residue into his body.

While a group of women administered to Cray, another unwrapped Sanders' sling and took off her top. Seeing her shoulder, one of them left and returned a few minutes later with a very long strip of weathered leather. The oldest woman in the group took it from her, wrapped one end twice around the left biceps, placed the leather strip over the clavicle, and anchored it to her torso in what doctors would call a perfect figure eight bandage. This held the clavicle tightly in place, allowing it to heal faster because it better immobilized the arm, something tribal women discovered over generations determining it was more effective and less painful than a sling.

Once the women finished administering their injuries, they removed the rest of Sanders' clothing and washed her and Cray from head-to-shoulder. Afterward, the older woman pointed for her to lay next to him. When she did, she covered them with a jaguar skin and motioned for her to sleep.

The LAR arrived at one in the afternoon without a captain or crew because Torres and Santiago had previously operated a similar craft. The ballistic-armored patrol boat weighed three tons, one and a half tons less than the lifting capacity of the UH-60 Black Hawk that transported the boat. It was twenty-five feet long, eight and a half feet wide, had a range of three hundred fifty miles, and could reach a speed of forty-five mph. Mounted on it were a 7.62 mm and a 12.7 mm machinegun, and a 40 mm grenade launcher.

Torres wasn't happy about it arriving so late in the day because, at most, they'd have four hours of daylight to find on which side of the tributary and where the canoe came ashore. Therefore, he wasn't optimistic about discovering the tribesman's village before nightfall.

The Black Hawk gently set the boat in the water and released the lifting straps securing it to the aircraft, afterward quickly gaining altitude with the heavy load no longer beneath it. Torres, who was in contact with the pilot, told him to bring his aircraft down and lower the rope ladder so they could transport his team to the LAR, which was fifteen feet from shore. That request brought a laugh from the pilot, who said he was low on fuel and wasn't going to waste time transporting ground pounders who didn't want to get wet.

"Look down," Torres said, surprising the pilot. Taking a packet of beef jerky from his backpack, he removed the beef strips and threw them into the water, the spot where they landed erupting in a feeding frenzy as hundreds of piranha tried getting to the dried meat.

"You made your point," the pilot said, lowering the Black Hawk while his crew chief unfolded the ladder.

Fifteen minutes later, the team was safely onboard. After stowing their gear, Torres sat at the controls with Santiago to his right.

"This place gives me the creeps," Santiago said out of earshot of the team.

"This chase is no different than the others. The Javari Valley is just another slice of the Amazon rainforest," Torres said. "The two civilians who walked through it made a mockery of its legends and superstitions."

"Until a headhunter captured them," Santiago reminded.

"Headhunters may be indigenous to the Javari Valley, but they're still locals. We've killed hundreds of villagers when someone wanted their land. Bows and arrows are no match for automatic weapons. When we encounter them, it will be a cakewalk."

Santiago didn't look reassured.

The woman came back to poke Cray every four hours, although no one in the village had a timepiece. The following day, he opened his eyes. Sanders, looking at him when he awoke, felt his forehead. His fever was nearly gone.

Looking under the jaguar skin, he saw they were naked. "What happened?" he asked, seeing her next to him. "The last thing I recall was you dragging me in a daze through the jungle."

Sanders told him what happened.

"No wonder my torso feels like a pin cushion. But whatever they did saved my life."

Before he could say anything further, one woman came forward and put a bowl of fruit, a gourd of water, and a bite of some type of protein beside Sanders, motioning for her to feed Cray.

"I don't know if they want us looking better before we're beheaded or if we're guests. For now, at least, we're alive," Sanders said.

"I think we're guests; otherwise, they wouldn't have bandaged your shoulder. Saving our captor's life might have something to do with how we're treated. However, we're about to repay that hospitality by putting their lives in grave danger because it's only a matter of time until the soldiers find the canoe and track us here. When they do, they'll kill me and everyone who knew I was here—which means you and the villagers."

"Who sent these soldiers after us?"

"I don't know."

"We have to tell the tribe."

"That's a given. With warning, they'll survive because they know this area so well and can escape in the brush and hide from them. We're the walking wounded. Barring something unforeseen, if these headhunters don't kill us, the soldiers will. We're not leaving the jungle alive."

"If you were at the top of your class in jungle survival training, you might have figured a way to save us," she said, kissing him on the lips while holding his hand.

"Dead last."

Torres' squad searched ten miles of shoreline on both sides of the tributary without finding where the canoe came ashore. They spent the night on the boat, expecting to be eaten alive by mosquitoes, which thrived in mineral-rich waters. However, in the morning, no one received a single bite. From experience, Torres knew that could only happen if the water had an acidic pH that kept the larvae from developing. That was the good news. The bad was that, without the tree canopy cover, they got pounded by rain for nearly three hours. Because the LAR was a military vessel, creature comforts were minimal, and there was no room to escape the deluge. Therefore, each person huddled under their poncho because ammunition, supplies, and water jugs took up the small amount of space below deck.

The following morning, Torres and Santiago put together a better way to find where the canoe came ashore. Knowing that Silva was the best person to spot an anomaly on the muddy shoreline, he maneuvered the shallow-draft boat as close to the bank as possible. Starting on the same side of the river where they'd seen the tribesman, they repeated their search from the previous day, again without success.

Torres saw Silva stumble and that he was slow getting back on his feet. He decided to take a one-hour break before searching the other bank, using this time to update Rocha. Three hours later, and with the sun beating down on the squad unmercifully, Silva yelled to stop the boat.

Torres brought the LAR to a stop and Santiago dropped the anchor.

"Look at the bank," Silva said, handing him the binoculars and pointing.

"I don't see anything. What am I looking for?"

"The area from the water's edge to the brush five yards away is smooth—something you don't see unless there's wave action. The tributary in this area is slow moving and calm, and this boat barely made a ripple on the shoreline."

"Your point?"

"This is the only bank on either side that's this smooth. The texture of the shore was impossible to notice yesterday in the dimming light, but in full sunlight, it's easy to see. Someone smoothed the ground to cover their tracks."

Torres marked the spot on his GPS and ordered the anchor pulled. "Move us a half mile upstream," he said to Santiago. "I don't want anyone from shore to see us. It's too early to go after them now, so we'll wait until dark to go ashore. Silva will lead the team and find the village, after which we'll move in and kill everyone. Once we photograph the bodies of the man and woman, we torch the place."

"How long until dark?" he asked Silva.

"Five hours and change."

"Have everyone clean their weapons, get some food, and grab some sleep," Torres told Santiago. "It's going to be a long night."

CHAPTER
TEN

Once Moretti left Camp David, the president ordered his VH-60N White Hawk helicopter, designated Marine One when he was onboard, to take him to Joint Base Andrews. Before leaving, he called the base's 89th Airlift Wing commander and told him that he was going to his office onboard Air Force One and would be there in less than thirty minutes.

The president arriving at his aircraft was common at the base, but not without significant advance notice. The typical presidential trip abroad took three months to plan, and three weeks if it was domestic, with the Secret Service making preparations well beforehand. Therefore, this visit caught the wing commander by surprise.

As with everything in the military, there was a checklist for just about any situation, and the base commander accessed his for fast-prepping Air Force One for static occupancy without a planned departure. The presidential hangar became a beehive of activity. Twenty-six minutes after receiving his call, the commander of the 89th saluted POTUS as he stepped off Marine One and escorted him to the ramp leading onto the 747-200B aircraft.

"I'd like a word with you in my office," the president said, surprising the colonel, who followed him onto the plane.

The president's private quarters were in the aircraft's nose. The suite included a bed, sofa, dressing room, bathroom, shower, and a small gym. Behind the suite was the president's office. Once inside, he asked the commander to have a seat in the chair in front of his desk.

"Colonel, what I'm about to say is top secret/SCI—president's eyes only information," Ballinger began.

"Understood, sir."

"I want you to generate an aircraft capable of HALO inserting a black ops team into Brazil. The pilot will receive precise coordinates from the team leader. Only you and the crew will know about this flight. The only record this base will have is that the aircraft will be going roundtrip to Brasilia, although the team's insertion won't be near there. After the drop, the aircraft will land for an indeterminate amount of time at two locations, which the team will give the pilot. I'll need you to get permission for their aircraft to land there without suspicion. The aircraft will return to Andrews from the second location with the team and two additional passengers."

The wing commander, who'd flown his share of TS/SCI missions, said he understood and asked the president to identify the two locations. The president did, saying the aircraft would wait at the first and transition to the second location for pickup following a call from the ops team.

"I'll ensure the aircraft has permission to land at both places. When will the team be here?"

"I expect them in less than thirty minutes," the president answered after looking at his watch. "Here's a list of the equipment which needs to be onboard the aircraft before they get here," he said, handing him Moretti's list.

"Holy shit!" the commander inadvertently responded, quickly apologizing afterward for his language.

"No apology necessary; just make it happen."

The colonel was on his cell phone before he stepped from the ramp onto the hangar floor. Summoning the on-call flight crew for the C-17 from the base alert facility, where crews for other aircraft were also on alert, he ordered them to get the State Department aircraft ready for wheels-up in less than twenty-five minutes.

Inserting an ops team into Brazil took creative thinking because he knew the Brazilians wouldn't permit a United States military aircraft to file a flight plan through their airspace. Therefore, the wing commander devised a plan using the State Department's C-17 transport, which was in a hangar at the base. For over a decade it had transported embassy pouches and diplomats, some of which were to Brasilia, where the US Embassy was located. However, according to the president, Brasilia wasn't near where the special ops team would drop. The ingenuity to get them there would need to come from the pilot.

The State Department had an ample supply of diplomatic pouches stored in the C-17's hangar. He ordered fifty to be taken to the base kitchen and gave them fifteen minutes to put cases of water inside and get them to the aircraft. He believed that this number of pouches would justify the use of an aircraft the size of the Globemaster III without creating suspicion when they left the plane in Brasilia.

The wing commander drove to the C-17's hangar, arriving the same time as the alert crew.

"Where to, colonel?" the pilot asked.

"Brasilia, where you'll deliver fifty diplomatic pouches. A black ops team will accompany you part of the way."

"Part of the way?" the aircraft commander asked.

"This is a top secret/SCI mission carrying a presidential designation, which means only five of us, besides the special ops team, know the orders you're about to receive."

Since the aircraft commander and crew had flown top secret/SCI missions in the past, they understood this designation meant they'd forget about it ever happening once they returned.

"The team will HALO," the colonel continued, referring to a high altitude, low opening parachute jump, "somewhere in Brazil at coordinates their team leader will provide. You'll also be dropping those," the commander said, pointing to a Zodiac and an equipment canister that a forklift was taking to the rear cargo door, followed by another forklift carrying the HALO gear and parachutes.

"Not a problem, sir. I've done something similar for special ops teams in the past," the aircraft commander replied. "I'll file a flight plan to Brasilia, change it en route and, at the appropriate time, report to air traffic control that a cargo door open light illuminated on my instrument panel requiring us to slow down and drop to a lower altitude to inspect the door. Once the team jumps, I'll advise ATC that it was a faulty indicator and ask to return to our original altitude and speed."

"That's a good plan."

"It's worked before."

"One last thing, you're not returning here from Brasilia. You'll be flying to two other locations, which the ops leader will provide."

The aircraft commander had been in the military long enough to know those locations wouldn't be remotely like Rio or Bali.

"Wheels up when they get here," the colonel concluded, shaking the hands of the crew, who then boarded the aircraft to do their preflight.

When the Nemesis team's helicopter arrived, the wing commander having told the tower to direct it to land behind the C-17 hangar, no one thought anything of it because the focus was on POTUS and the flurry of activity around Air Force One—which was the president's intent. Therefore, Moretti and his team walked unnoticed up the cargo ramp with their backpacks and weapons in hand. The flight crew, who were in their seats waiting for their arrival, went to the rear of the aircraft when they heard the team's helicopter land and greeted each operative as they stepped onboard.

Moretti had deployed on over a dozen missions where he gave the pilot their destination once he stepped onto the aircraft. In each case, he didn't verbally give them the coordinates. Instead, to avoid a misunderstanding that would mean his team was jumping into the wrong area, he handed them a slip of paper on which he wrote the drop coordinates. He did the same with the pilot of the C-17.

Once the crew returned to the cockpit, the team checked the Zodiac, seeing that extra gas containers were inside, as Moretti requested. Next, they inspected their HALO gear, ensuring the oxygen tanks had enough gas to get them from twenty-five thousand feet to below fifteen thousand without suffocating. After checking their masks to see if they were getting an adequate flow of oxygen, they placed their backpacks and weapons in the equipment canister and told the crew chief they were good to go.

The C-17, with a length of one hundred seventy-four feet and a wingspan of one hundred sixty-nine feet, was airborne before it was a third down the eleven thousand three hundred feet long runway. Although neither the team nor crew could see him, the president had left Air Force One and was standing on the tarmac looking at the Globemaster III lift off, continuing to watch as it faded into the distance.

The flight to Brazil was uneventful, with the team sleeping most of the way knowing that once they jumped, rest would be a scarce commodity. Because the coordinates that Moretti gave the aircraft commander weren't on the way to Brasilia, when the aircraft was close to Brazilian airspace, the pilot amended the flight plan for a course that took the Globemaster through the Javari Valley. Air traffic control didn't care about the longer route because their flightpath didn't go through restricted airspace, feeling if those onboard the diplomatic aircraft wanted to sightsee, it was their fuel to burn. Therefore, ATC approved the revised flight plan as filed. The pilot would use his ruse to get the aircraft down to twenty-five thousand feet just before the team jumped.

An hour from insertion, Moretti received a call from Alexson giving him new coordinates for the LAR. Copying these down, he walked into the cockpit and handed the revised drop point to the aircraft commander. The pilot took the paper and entered the new coordinates into the navigation system.

"We're talking a change of three miles. It shouldn't be a problem amending our flight plan with ATC," the pilot said. "When I'm near, I'll say my radar shows bad weather ahead and ask to circumvent it. Whatever their response, I'll put your team over the jump point." The co-pilot and crew chief were listening.

"Because this is a diplomatic aircraft," the crew chief interjected, "we don't have jump lights. All instructions will come from me."

Moretti said he understood.

"Is twenty-five thousand feet good for your drop?" the pilot asked, knowing it was the altitude most often used for a HALO.

"That will be perfect. It sounds like you've done this before."

"I flew MC-130 aircraft out of the 8th Special Operations Squadron at Hurlburt Field, Florida."

Moretti visibly relaxed, knowing he had a special ops pilot at the controls.

"You already know this, but I'll still go over what will happen, so there's no misunderstanding," the pilot continued.

"Misunderstandings get you killed," Moretti said, drawing a nod from the flight crew.

"Five minutes prior to your jump, I'll declare that I have a door open light with ATC, significantly decreasing the speed of the aircraft to one hundred and seventy. As I slow down, I'll depressurize the plane and my crew chief will lower the rear cargo door. Five seconds before we get to your coordinates, I'll tell him to release the Zodiac. Once that goes, everyone follows."

"I saw the Zodiac has the JPADS system attached to it, as I requested," Moretti said, referring to the joint position airdrop system that used GPS, a steerable parachute, and an onboard computer system to steer loads to a designated impact point.

"We've used this system several times before. My co-pilot will guide the Zodiac to the coordinates you gave me. We're fifty-eight minutes away from your jungle cruise."

The change in coordinates that Moretti gave the aircraft commander came from an NSA intercept of a conversation between Torres and Rocha after Silva discovered where the tribesman's canoe came ashore. Since Moretti planned to take out Torres' squad after they'd led the Nemesis team to Cray and the plus one while avoiding becoming a headhunter's trophy, he felt more confident now that Torres better defined Cray's location. Besides the techies at Site R, during the flight, Moretti was in contact with the commander of the 89th, who needed to coordinate the C-17's two other landing locations.

Once they rescued Cray and his companion, the plan was to get into the Zodiac and go like a bat out of hell to Leticia, Colombia, which was one hundred seven miles away. Six hundred twenty-one miles inland from there was Apiay, an airbase that the United States shared with the Colombian Air Force to support their drug interdiction efforts. Following Brasilia, the C-17 would wait there for Moretti's call. After receiving it, it'd fly to the Alfredo Vasquez Cabo Airport in Leticia, whose asphalt runway was sixty-one hundred feet, twenty-six hundred feet more than the Globemaster needed. Since the United States had a revolving door of special ops types coming in and out of Colombia on US military aircraft, for which the Colombians didn't keep a record, the commander of the 89th Airlift Wing asked his counterpart in Apiay for permission to land the Globemaster there and at the commercial airport in Leticia. He approved those requests on the assumption it was another special ops mission.

Moretti knew this plan, which of necessity was a last minute endeavor, had the adhesiveness of a Post-it Note. But given there was no way to exfil from an airstrip in Brazil, Colombia was their only way out.

However, what subsequently happened was a far cry from what he planned, his Post-it Note blown away with the ferocity of a category four hurricane.

Twenty minutes before the cargo door opened, the team slipped on their high-altitude flight suit, opened their oxygen valve, and donned ballistic helmets with night vision goggles. Each HALO suit had a navigation unit attached to the left sleeve, which they programmed with the last coordinates Moretti gave the pilot. After clipping on their oxygen mask, they tightly strapped themselves into their webbed seats, knowing what was to follow. The equipment canister, which contained weapons and backpacks, was beside Moretti.

The crew chief, wearing a heavy flight jacket and a helmet with a portable oxygen tank, walked through the cargo compartment, ensuring that everything was secure so it wouldn't blow through the cargo compartment during depressurization. He then strapped himself into the seat closest to the cargo door, which was next to its control panel, and told the pilot that he and the team were good to go. In response, the aircraft commander said they were two minutes and ten seconds from depressurization.

Ten seconds later, the C-17's co-pilot reported their fictitious problem to Brazilian air traffic control as the pilot slowed the aircraft and began the plane's descent to twenty-five thousand feet. Upon reaching that altitude, he depressurized the aircraft and lowered the cargo ramp. Instantaneously, there was a loud bang as the high-pressure air burst from the aircraft into the low-pressure surroundings outside. With the aircraft's rear open, the temperature dropped from seventy to fifty degrees Fahrenheit, with that differential turning the moisture within the cargo compartment into a fog.

Immediately after depressurization, the crew chief pulled the release lever for the Zodiac. Once free, the lower outside air pressure sucked the craft out of the plane, the static line attached to it releasing the steerable parachutes of the JPADS system. With the Zodiac out of their way, the team didn't wait for an invitation. In practiced precision, they unfastened their seat harnesses and leaped off the cargo ramp into the pitch black opening with Moretti, who had the equipment canister, the last to go.

Because the air at twenty-five thousand feet was thinner than at lower altitudes, their freefall speed topped two hundred mph. Moretti, attached to the heavy equipment canister, had a slightly faster descent. Focused on their navigation unit, each person made minute adjustments to ensure they'd hit their landing area. If they didn't, they'd be in the two hundred feet high jungle canopy surrounding it.

They pulled their parachute's release cord at three thousand feet, extended their elbows and hands, opened their legs, and flattened their gut to create aerodynamic drag and slow down. Moretti was the first to land on the bank of the tributary, disconnecting his canister just before touching down. The rest of the team followed a couple of seconds later, everyone landing as gently as if they were walking on a carton of eggs. Twenty feet ahead of them was the FC 470 Zodiac with twin 150-hp Evinrude 2-stroke engines that propelled the craft to fifty-two mph. The co-pilot had nailed the landing onto the narrow bank of wet earth.

After discarding their HALO gear, the team removed their backpacks and weapons from the canister and inserted magazines into their .45-cal Heckler & Koch MK23 handgun and Heckler & Koch 9mm MP5 submachine gun. Jian Shen, the team's marksman, carried an additional gun—the QBU-88 sniper rifle. Each weapon had a suppressor attached to it.

Every member of the team wore a Boonie hat, the government designation for a bucket hat, under which was a headset mic. Strapped to their wrists was a Garmin Foretrex® 401 handheld GPS receiver. The slim waterproof device had an LCD screen, electronic compass, and stored up to five hundred waypoints, ten tracks with ten thousand points, allowing one to retrace their path back to the starting point.

"Let's get the Zodiac in the water," Moretti said, not wasting any time.

After unfastening the JPADS system, they pushed it to the bank's edge. With McGough standing at the front of the Zodiac, the team dragged the three hundred fifty pounds craft into two feet of water. Immediately, McGough jumped, grabbed his leg, and ran back to shore. Looking down, he saw pieces of his pants legs were missing and a piranha was clinging to his pocket. Grabbing the center of the fish, he tossed it back into the water. The gashes in his legs, while bleeding, weren't severe. After removing the first aid kit from his backpack, he patched himself with antibacterial ointment and a waterproof bandage.

This time, everyone pushed the Zodiac from the rear, getting in when it was three-quarters of the way into the water and using the paddles to move away from shore. Looking at the coordinates of the LAR on his GPS receiver, Moretti started the craft in that direction. Eighteen minutes later, the team had it in sight.

CHAPTER
ELEVEN

The squad was awake and eating their rations. No one spoke, reflecting their nervousness about attacking a headhunter village. Even though they were the only ones with firearms, they had never confronted a headhunter tribe. They'd had enough jungle experience to know the disadvantage of being on someone else's turf, and if they lost the element of surprise, they'd never make it out of this jungle alive.

Torres removed the cover over the luminous dial on his watch, noting the time. "Gear up," he said, seeing that everyone had finished their rations, and wanting to get started earlier than he originally planned because he could see the nervousness in his men's faces and knew that waiting would only worsen their anxiety. "You know what we have to do. Once we find the village, we'll execute a pincer movement, with Santiago's team on one end and mine on the other. Let's do this and get out of here. Remember, there will be no survivors." He engaged the engines and headed for the spot where Silva had said the canoe came ashore.

Through their night vision goggles, the Nemesis team saw the LAR beached a hundred yards ahead, silently putting their paddles in the water as they slowly approached its stern. Twenty feet away, they stowed their paddles and let their craft glide to it. Han Li was the first on board, grabbing onto the Brazilian vessel and soundlessly stepping on deck, followed by the rest of the team. With their suppressed handguns pointed in front of them, and night vision goggles over their eyes, they searched the vessel.

"They've gone," Han Li said, summarizing their disappointment.

"McGough. You and Shen untie the Zodiac and move it upstream on the other side of that fallen tree where no one can see it," Moretti said, pointing to a spot thirty yards away. "The rest of us will look for their trail."

When they returned, they found the rest of the team standing around numerous boots prints that went into a slit in the vegetation.

"I'll take the lead," Moretti said as he entered the tiny opening, with Han Li following.

"Why am I not thrilled about going in there?" Bonaquist asked as he followed her.

The answer to that question appeared a hundred yards into the vegetation when he saw a *false fer-de-lance* snake coiled in front and to the side of Moretti, Han Li putting a bullet into the thirty-one inches long reptile.

"Be careful where you step," Moretti said into his mic, alerting those in the rear, although given where they were, that warning was unnecessary.

As they continued following the trampled vegetation, the animal cries from around them got louder. Given the height of the vegetation, something as large as a jaguar could hide feet away, and they'd never see it until it was too late. Fifty yards from where Han Li put a bullet in the *fer-de-lance,* Moretti saw movement in the vegetation. He pushed aside a plant with the tip of his rifle, saw a coral snake, and put a round in it.

"It looks like the predators think Uber Eats just got here," Bonaquist said. "Look twenty feet up in the tree at two o'clock."

Everyone did, seeing a jaguar staring at them.

"Jian, scare it away from us," Moretti said.

Shen shot a round into the branch on which the jaguar crouched, an inch from its front leg. The apex predator, not used to being threatened, scurried up the tree and out of sight.

As they continued, a tarantula came off a large leaf that Shen brushed against and walked onto his backpack. McGough, behind him, took the tip of his rifle and flicked it off, Shen never knowing what happened. Two hundred yards further, they saw one of Torres' men lying on his back with his eyes open.

Torres slowed his team to a crawl after losing one of his squad to an unidentified snake, which slithered into the vegetation after biting its victim. He believed the extremely narrow path they were on led to the village because Silva told him the compactness of the ground and the extensive broken vegetation beside them showed people had walked on it for decades. Since they were in the middle of nowhere, he surmised an indigenous village was the only logical destination. Torres wasn't one for blind trust, but he didn't have a choice in the jungle. Silva was the only person with the skills to navigate them through the thick jungle growth, especially at night, following tracking signs that would go unnoticed by others, find the village, and get them back to their boat. One hundred yards later, they exited the vegetation and saw the shabono.

Implementing their plan of attack, two of the team followed Santiago to the left while he led the rest to the right. On his signal, both teams, wearing night vision goggles, burst into the shabono. Upon entering, each member ripped off a clip of ammo, peppering the interior with their high-velocity rounds without looking for a specific target. The pungent smell of nitroglycerin from their ammo was strong as they reloaded before looking at the carnage they'd unleashed.

"Merda!" Torres exclaimed.

The shabono was empty. They'd walked into a trap.

Hiding in the dense vegetation ten yards from the shabono, the Nemesis team heard automatic gunfire from multiple weapons.

"Wait for the Brazilian squad to come out. When they do, take them down," Moretti said, his voice angry with resolve, believing they'd slaughtered those inside the structure, possibly including Cray and the plus one. Therefore, he thought they deserved the same consideration.

Then it happened. Jian Shen felt a sharp prick in his neck. Reaching back, he pulled out the wooden dart and felt the remnants of the sticky black paste on the tip. Traveling at four hundred feet per second, twice the velocity of an arrow from a wooden self-bow, the razor-sharp tip easily penetrated his skin. As the poison coursed through his body, he felt dizzy and confused, having difficulty ordering his brain to do the most basic functions. What happened next caused the ordinarily unflappable sniper to panic when his limbs became paralyzed and his breathing labored. Dropping his weapon because he could no longer grip it, he fell to his knees and onto his side as he heard slowly approaching footsteps.

Bonaquist was next to be struck by a dart, followed by McGough, Moretti, and then Han Li. As with Shen, all became disabled and lay on the ground dying, the Shuars squatting beside them, waiting for the poison to take their lives.

"Let's do this," Torres said, deciding they were sitting ducks inside the shabono and needed to leave before the natives set it on fire or daylight arrived. With night vision goggles and automatic weapons, he felt they had the advantage if they got out quickly and returned to their boat.

The squad bolted from the thatched opening closest to the trail, firing a fusillade of bullets in a two hundred seventy degree arc to cover their escape. Whether it was the sound of them running or just luck, the six surviving squad members went through the narrow slit of vegetation without being bitten or eaten by a predator. When they arrived at the LAR, they wasted no time pushing the stern deeper into the water and climbing onto the vessel. The engine started on command, and Torres began reversing the craft into the tributary. Because there was a new moon, meaning the side of the moon facing earth received no direct sunlight and was not visible to the unaided eye, the entire area was pitch black. To Torres, that meant the headhunters couldn't follow them as their dugout canoes were no match for the speed of the LAR.

"We made it," Torres said to Santiago. However, a moment later, he discovered the fallacy of that statement after seeing their boat sinking. Because the source of the leak wasn't obvious, and he couldn't go into the piranha-infested waters to inspect the hull, he rammed the engine to full forward throttle and beached the LAR.

The squad jumped off the boat, Torres ordering four of his men to stand guard while he and Santiago searched for the leak, hoping they could fix it while the four killed any approaching tribesman.

It took less than a minute to find that the water entering the vessel was coming through a breach in the bow just below the waterline.

"It looks as if someone took an ax to the hull," Santiago said to Torres, who was standing beside him.

"We'll plug the hole with lifejackets and hold them in place with duct tape," Torres replied. "That will last long enough to put some distance between this tribe and us. I'll call Rocha and have him airlift us out at daylight."

As they began wedging the lifejackets into the rough opening, all hell broke loose. Silva was the first to die, taking an arrow in the heart. Seeing this, the three soldiers beside him responded by indiscriminately spraying the jungle with a barrage of bullets. While reloading, an arrow found each.

"How in the hell can they see us?" Torres asked, not expecting an answer. "Take the grenade launcher and pulverize the fringe area of the jungle," he said, as he pressed the last piece of duct tape over the lifejackets.

That never happened because no sooner had he said this than an arrow struck Santiago in the throat. As he was suffocating on his blood, Torres returned to the boat and pushed him aside to get at the controls. Gunning the engine in reverse, he re-entered the water as arrows arched harmlessly into the water short of the LAR.

Torres opened the emergency bilge ejection value to pump the accumulated water overboard and pushed the throttle to full power. The boat should have taken off like a horse in the Kentucky Derby. Instead, it was moving like it was in a sea of molasses.

Running below deck, he saw that the height of the water hadn't gone down. Instead, it was higher, meaning his patch didn't hold and he was sinking. As he stepped below deck to patch the leak again, he felt an intense biting pain in both legs. Knowing what caused it, he jumped from the water and returned topside, where he saw he was bleeding from large gouges torn in his skin. Since returning to the bank where the tribe was slinging arrows at him wasn't an option, he turned the LAR around and headed for the opposite shore. Thirty yards away, his engine stopped.

With the boat continuing to get lower in the water, he thought his only chance to survive was to create a diversion and swim like hell for shore. He was a strong swimmer and could get there in less than half a minute. After putting his satphone in a plastic bag and stuffing it into his pocket and ensuring his night vision goggles were secure on his head, he removed his boots. He then picked up Santiago and heaved him into the water. As expected, the area around the body churned with piranha creating what he hoped would be a lengthy diversion.

The first ten yards went better than expected, with only a nibble or two on his torso and limbs. The next ten were considerably more painful when the piranha, averaging twelve inches in length and weighing two pounds, sensed the blood from his wounds and made a beeline to him. Because piranha grouped in schools of twenty to thirty, and thousands of schools were in that area of the tributary, there wasn't a piece of Torres' flesh that was visible beneath the hundreds of piranha that attached to him, each with outsized jaw muscles that exerted a bite force of thirty times their bodyweight. Knowing he was slowly being eaten alive and there was nothing he could do, he opened his mouth, hoping to drown and end his agony quickly. However, downing isn't immediate, and it wasn't until thirty seconds later that death occurred. Ten minutes after that, his skeletal remains settled at the bottom of the tributary, not far from Santiago and the final resting place of the LAR.

"He's coming around," Cray said to Sanders as they looked down at Moretti, who was lying on a mat in the shabono beside the other Nemesis members. A woman from the tribe, who was caring for him, helped the ex-Ranger sit up and gave him something to drink before stepping away.

"What happened?" Moretti asked in an uneven voice. Looking around, he saw Cray and Sanders. Standing behind them and looking intently at him was the tribe, most of the men with shrunken heads hanging around their waists.

Cray helped Moretti sit up.

"How are you both alive?"

As the rest of the team began to awake, each reacted similarly to seeing the couple, believing them to be dead.

"I first want to learn how you knew we were in trouble and found us. Was it after you discovered the floatplane didn't return to the charter company?" Cray asked.

"Neither the company nor the media reported your plane missing."

That surprised Cray and Sanders. "Then how? he asked. "We're in the middle of the rainforest without my satcom signal or the benefit of satellite imagery."

"Why aren't our heads, or yours, adorning the waists of those looking at us?" Moretti asked instead.

"Before I answer, let me introduce my fiancé, Erin Sanders," Cray said with a smile, knowing the reaction he'd get.

"Fiancé?"

Cray sat on the mat next to Moretti. When his future wife sat beside him, he put his arm over her shoulder. The remaining four team members assembled around the three as Cray told their story, spellbinding everyone.

"And you believe they spared your lives because you saved a member of the tribe from the Brazilian soldiers?" Han Li asked.

"I don't see another explanation."

"How did you know they were going to attack the village?"

"I knew I was the target when our floatplane was being shot at by someone in uniform and followed through the jungle by soldiers who began shooting at me. Someone in Brazil's military wanted me dead and, if they went to the trouble of finding my charter flight and inserting soldiers with the skills to follow me through this unforgiving rainforest, I was certain they would not give up until they killed me. Therefore, I had no doubt they would track me here. I also believed they would kill Erin and everyone in the tribe to avoid witnesses."

Moretti nodded in agreement.

"How did you convey this to the tribe since you don't speak their language?" Moretti asked.

"We drew images in the dirt to illustrate what each said. It took hours, but eventually, I could see from his facial expressions and drawings that he understood the meaning of what I was depicting. The same applied to his images. Once we established a way to communicate, he understood my concerns about the Brazilian soldiers. He spoke to that person, who appears to be their leader," Cray continued, pointing to Proud Bird.

"Give me an example of these drawings," Moretti asked.

Cray picked up a nearby stick, moved part of the mat aside, and began drawing in the hard earth. "This is our symbol for a friend, this for an enemy, and this is the graphic for their tribe," he said.

"And after he understood the village was going to be attacked by soldiers?" Bonaquist asked with anticipation.

"He spoke to the tribe, and the men began grabbing bows, quivers filled with arrows, blowguns, and pouches containing darts. We then went into the jungle to wait for the soldiers to arrive."

"And they didn't know we were friendlies," Han Li stated.

"No, which is why you almost died. I'm speculating that to the tribe, an intruder is an intruder. Therefore, there's no difference between the Brazilian soldiers and Nemesis. Since the bad guys were inside the hut, you were an easy target, and they quickly killed you," Cray said, miming quotation marks with both hands when he said killed. "Putting aside my shock at the team being here, I was frantic when I saw what happened and signaled the young tribesman that you were friends by placing my hands over my heart and pointing to all of you. We'd used this same gesture in the past, and I mimicked it."

"We were lucky they had an antidote to the poison," McGough said.

Cray said the young tribesman removed a small piece of leather from his dart pouch, and inside was a paste that he put on your wounds and under your tongues. "I'm guessing the men keep this antidote in their dart pouches in case they accidentally prick themself with either a poison arrow or dart."

""That makes sense. Your quick thinking saved our lives," Han Li stated. "Let's segue. How did the two of you fall in love while going through a rainforest filled with predators, chased by soldiers, and brought to the communal living area of a headhunter village?"

Cray explained from his perspective, and Sanders followed with her viewpoint. From the way they spoke, no one doubted the two were deeply in love.

"When did he pop the question?" Moretti asked.

"Yesterday, as we were lying together and talking. One thing led to another, and before long, we decided we wanted to spend our lives together."

"Did you know beforehand?"

"I suspected he wanted us to be a couple from how he looked at me and kept using the word "we" instead of "I" as we went through the jungle. That became more of a certainty when he said that, if we survived, he wanted me to move into his house. But I didn't know he wanted to get married until he popped the question."

Cray interrupted. "Neither of us have been married nor lived with someone. However, even though we'd only known each other for a few days, I said I was never more certain of anything than spending the rest of my life with her. She said she felt the same."

"Beautiful," Han Li stated.

"Let's get back to how you knew we were in trouble, found us, and got here," Cray said.

"Libby Parra," Moretti replied and explained.

CHAPTER
TWELVE

Colonel Henrique Rocha assumed he had a problem when he didn't hear from Torres in the morning. That feeling amplified when he failed to reach him or the other squad members on their satcom phones. The military didn't regard no news as good news. However, he understood that because the squad was in the jungle, there were logical reasons for this lack of contact. Torres was possibly still after the Cray, the villagers, or both and couldn't communicate because he was below the thick jungle canopy. Another possibility was that, because they were in the Javari Valley, an area for which no maps existed, they were lost or had a negative encounter with a tribe—meaning they were dead.

Since waiting wasn't his strong suit, Rocha needed a helicopter to find the LAR for his peace of mind, if nothing else. That would, at least, give him some idea of the approximate location of his men. Standing in the way of him doing this was that he was only authorized to use rotary and fixed-wing aircraft for insertions and logistical support. Therefore, if he wanted a helicopter to search for his team, he needed Vilar's help.

The call with his counterpart went as expected. Vilar, who was keenly interested in not joining Rocha in front of a firing squad if their mercenary business came to light, said he would go to the Javari Valley with his pilot to look for the craft and take whatever action was necessary if he encountered Cray and his plus one.

Vilar knew that Cray and the person he was with could never leave the jungle alive. They'd seen him shoot down their floatplane and Torres' squad try to kill them. From what Bradford said about the American's connection to the president of the United States, he had more than enough influence to get the US government to launch a real investigation, not one that was superficial with a predetermined outcome. Although his government might not be on the best terms with America, the president of Brazil wasn't about to let two colonels embarrass his country on the world stage by making nations believe their military had pockets of mercenaries embedded in it. A call from one head of state to the other, and it was over.

After logging his flight as a request from Rocha to continue searching for the crash victims of the character aircraft, Vilar ordered the M-35M Hind helicopter that was at the Manaus Air Force Base to be prepped for flight because the UH-60 Black Hawk he'd used to blow the floatplane from the sky was down for maintenance. The nine-ton Russian-manufactured helicopter, modified for extended range, had a twin-barrel 23mm cannon under its chin and carried a pod of 80mm unguided rockets beneath each stubby wing. Within thirty minutes of getting Rocha's call, Vilar was on his way to Manaus with his pilot at the controls. Along the way, he spoke with Bradford.

"I'm not interested in excuses," Carter texted Bradford over Tor. "Your first assumption was that Cray died in the crash. He didn't. The next was that he wouldn't survive in the rainforest. He has. Your third baseless claim was that the Brazilian kill squad would murder him and the woman he's with, a person we still know nothing about. They haven't. Now you're telling me they won't survive their capture by a headhunter. My response is they will because your assumptions have continually proved incorrect. Let me be clear. Stop making assumptions. I want to see their bodies." Their communication abruptly ended.

Bradford knew Carter was right. He'd made assumptions

based on what someone thought; finding out the hard way this information was wishful thinking. His call with Vilar had him especially concerned because Rocha had lost contact with the squad. That meant he didn't know the current situation. Looking at a digital map of the Javari Valley, he saw the spot on the tributary where Rocha said they dropped the LAR. It was only a hundred miles from Leticia, Colombia. If Cray and his plus one made it there, a call to his boss and he'd have a VIP flight back to the States.

Killing Cray in the jungle for what he may or may not know, as Carter wanted, was one thing. However, if he somehow made it out of the jungle and spoke with the president, the subsequent investigation by the acting or a newly appointed FBI director, or those within the Bureau over whom he had no influence, would expose Vilar and Rocha. The Brazilian colonels would give him up in a New York minute to save their skins. Therefore, he would no longer give them the autonomy to handle the situation. The FBI had a long reach in South America. With the acting director just getting his feet wet, and as the director of the Bureau's intel division, with the right story, he'd get him to grant access to whatever resources he needed.

Thinking about it, the story he'd use would be that his intel revealed that a group of extremely dangerous terrorists was going to enter Colombia from Brazil, using a drug cartel's underground network to get them into the United States. Because the FBI had over eighty overseas locations, one of which was in Bogota, he'd go to that field office and say that he'd received credible intel that these terrorists were sneaking into Colombia from Brazil using a remote tributary of the Amazon River. Because the FBI considered them extremely dangerous, he would request the Colombian military to accompany agents from the Bogota office, suggest the use of deadly force by their troops, and recommend cordoning off the tributary around Leticia.

When Bradford got to the El Dorado International Airport in Bogota the following morning, he went to the FBI field office and saw the agent in charge. Getting straight to the point, he handed him photos of Cray and the other members of Nemesis, identifying them as terrorists. He omitted their names and that they worked for the White House. He also said that a woman, whose photo he didn't have, was accompanying them.

"You must have good intel," the head of the office said, spreading the pictures on his desk. "None of our sources, normally very reliable, gave us a clue of their arrival. I'll run these photos through our database and see if they're in our system."

"There's no need. I ran them through the Homeland Security photo recognition system and came up empty."

"You know we can't operate on Colombian soil without the government's permission."

"We can't stop these terrorists without the help of their military."

"We have a military liaison in this office."

Bradford knew this. "Whatever we say between us and the military liaison must be strictly confidential. I don't want a paper or digital trail on meetings, what we said, and so forth. When this operation is over, it never happened."

The agent in charge agreed and didn't believe the Colombians would object. He left his office and returned several minutes later with a Colombian Army major. Bradford introduced himself and handed him his business card and a set of photos, adding that he didn't have a picture of the woman accompanying them. From the expression on the major's face on seeing the director's card, that didn't matter. He seemed flattered to be speaking with someone so senior at the Bureau.

"They're going to enter Colombia?" the major asked.

"US intelligence believes they're in Brazil and coming up a tributary of the Amazon River to Leticia. We don't know exactly when, but we believe it will be soon. Assuming we stop them on the tributary, I'm assuming the Colombian government wouldn't want to pay the court and incarceration costs for these terrorists," Bradford said.

"Terrorists are like cockroaches. If you don't kill them, they multiply, and the infestation becomes overwhelming. We'll block the tributary at Leticia, inspecting all traffic coming from Brazil," the major said. "I'll have these photos copied and distributed to the military installation nearby. When these terrorists arrive, we'll be ready."

"Leticia is a little over a hundred miles from here—straight down the tributary in that direction," Moretti told Cray as he pointed northwest. "It's where Brazil, Colombia, and Peru come together in an area called Tres Fronteras. We'll be there in two hours once I'm at full throttle. I called the C-17 aircraft commander. He'll be waiting for us at the Leticia airport, which is three miles from the docks."

"How do we get between the two?" Cray asked.

"I have US dollars. I'll hotwire a car if all else fails and no one wants to take our money. No matter what, we're getting on that aircraft."

As the other team members began sliding the Zodiac into the water, Cray looked at the tribe, who were at the water's edge staring at the strange craft in which the intruders would depart. An hour earlier, Cray had communicated to Shining Anaconda that he was releasing him from his obligation. As a gift, he gave the young tribesman his ratchet belt. He immediately took the shrunken heads off the rope around his waist and placed them on it. Moretti offered his to Proud Bird, which pleased the elder, who also moved his trophies to it.

With Moretti at the controls, the Zodiac backed away from shore and turned towards Leticia, gradually increasing speed until it was zipping along at close to fifty mph. Those within hunkered down, Moretti being the only exception as he deftly kept the craft in the center of the waterway, whose direction frequently twisted and turned. Since he had his hands full controlling the craft at this speed, Han Li phoned the C-17 pilot and gave him their current position and expected arrival time, learning they were already airborne from

Apiay to Leticia. Knowing the transport aircraft was on its way to get them, everyone on the Zodiac relaxed, confident that their ordeal was nearly over.

The first sign of trouble occurred when Moretti, who had 20/15 vision, saw the outline of what he knew was a low-flying M-35 Hind on the horizon. "That's a military helicopter," the ex-Ranger said, pointing to it.

Although it took a few seconds because no one had better than 20/20 vision, everyone eventually saw the outline of the Russian-built helicopter.

"Didn't you say a military helicopter shot down your floatplane?" Han Li asked.

"A Black Hawk. That's a Hind, which has even greater firepower," Cray answered, holding tightly onto his fiancé in the fast-moving craft. "How far to Leticia?"

"Thirty miles," McGough answered, looking at the numbers on his Garmin GPS receiver.

"That means we're close to the Colombian border. Let's hope the Hind is on patrol," Bonaquist stated as the helicopter rapidly approached.

"What the …?" Moretti said, seeing a burst of rockets streaking towards them from one of the helicopter's underwing pods. He pulled back the power to idle. Moments later, the rockets impacted the water where the Zodiac would have been if he had maintained his course and speed. He again pushed the throttles to the max.

"Those are either S-8 or S-13 unguided rockets. They're point and shoot," Cray said.

"There's more in those pods," Bonaquist volunteered.

"Forget about the rockets," Cray countered. "Worry about the twin 23mm cannons in the front. They're deadly-effective within a mile."

"You know a lot about this helicopter," Sanders said.

"The Russians sold these to our adversaries, and they were always hammering us in the Middle East."

"I encountered Hinds in both Iraq and Afghanistan," McGough volunteered. "Once those guns get within range, they'll shred this boat."

"What's the range of our guns?" Sanders asked, looking at the MP5 submachine guns the team carried.

"One-fifth of the twin 23mm cannons on that beast."

"Damn."

The Hind pilot didn't waste any more rockets. Instead, he maneuvered his aircraft fifty feet over the jungle canopy and closed the distance to the Zodiac to eight hundred yards. He took his time getting into position because he was six hundred yards beyond the range of small arms fire. Therefore, with each of his two cannons firing at a rate of three thousand six hundred rounds a minute, it would only take a quick pull of the trigger to rip the Zodiac and everyone inside to pieces.

Swinging his cannons to starboard, the pilot pointed them toward the fast-moving craft, which was zip-zagging across the water. He viewed this maneuver as meaningless because he could walk the massive stream of bullets, which traveled at three thousand two hundred fifteen feet per second, across the water until they struck the boat. Game over. "By your command," he said to Vilar.

"Kill them."

CHAPTER
THIRTEEN

A C-17 Globemaster III has an empty weight of two hundred eighty-two thousand five hundred pounds. Add one hundred eighty-one thousand pounds of fuel, and it weighs just over two hundred thirty-one tons without cargo. In contrast, a Hind weighs twelve tons. Therefore, when the Globemaster flew over it, clearing its blades by mere feet, each of the vortices from the C-17's wings struck the heavily armored tandem-seat helicopter with a force not unlike an eighteen-wheeler hitting a passenger car. This downward-swirling air violently pushed the Hind into the jungle canopy at nearly three hundred feet per second, far too fast for the pilot to react.

On impact, the stubby wings, which held the rocket pods, tore away and the fuselage split apart directly behind the pilot. Because the nose of the aircraft was heavy—housing the twin cannons, its ammunition, and the cockpit's electronics, it dropped straight down, breaking branch after branch as it plummeted one hundred eighty feet until it hit the jungle floor, killing the pilot.

In contrast, Vilar's section of the fuselage was far lighter and wedged tightly in thick branches. Uninjured, he unfastened his five-point harness and was about to descend branch-by-branch from the twenty stories tall tree when he heard a growl thirty feet below. Looking down, he saw a giant jaguar staring at him. Beside the apex predator were two tiny cubs. Vilar froze in fear as he watched the predator gracefully leap from branch to branch until it was beside him. At that moment, he understood he would be the next meal for the mother and her cubs.

Those on the Zodiac cheered when they saw the C-17 pilot destroy the Hind. After Moretti cut the throttles to bring the boat to a stop, he called the aircraft commander on his satphone, putting their conversation on speaker. However, before he could thank him for saving their lives and ask why he was here and not waiting for them at the Leticia airport, the pilot told him the conversations he heard from those at the airbase in Apiay, after which he and the crew decided to keep an eye on them.

"The Colombians can call the White House and find out we're not terrorists," Moretti volunteered.

"From what I heard, the Colombian Navy isn't going to ask you questions, nor want to see your passports or ID cards. They believe you're all terrorists trying to sneak into their country and intend to blow your Zodiac out of the water as soon as they see it."

"This body of water only goes in two directions. If we return the way we came, there's nothing but jungle, and we'll run out of gas. If we continue toward Leticia, you're saying the Colombian navy will kill us."

"You could call the president and have him speak to the president of Colombia," the pilot volunteered. "That would end the blockade and get you a safe passage."

"That's not an option we can use," Moretti countered. "Those on the Colombian vessel will see that we're coming from Brazilian waters. I can't take a chance that one of them will leak what they saw, especially when they're called off by the president of their country. If the Brazilian government discovered the US put boots on their soil without permission, it would strain Brazil-America relations greatly. We need to find a stealthy way to get past the blockade."

"I might have a solution," the pilot said, "but I can't guarantee the outcome won't be the same."

"It could hardly be worse. What is it?"

The pilot told him.

"I was wrong," Moretti said.

Bradford concluded that being an armchair quarterback wasn't in his best interests, and he needed to be closer to the action. Therefore, he accompanied the liaison officer to Leticia on a Colombian Air Force plane. On the flight, the major received word from the commander of the ship blockading the tributary that a US diplomatic flight traveling from Colombia to Brazil spotted the wreckage of a rigid-hulled craft on that same branch of the Amazon, but in Brazilian territory. The captain went on to say that the aircraft commander had informed Brazilian and Colombian air traffic controls, giving them the coordinates for the debris field.

"Since the wreckage is in Brazilian waters, we can't go there without their permission."

"I must confirm if this was the terrorist's boat," Bradford told the major. "If it isn't, and the Navy abandons the blockade, those terrorists could enter Colombia, and from there, the United States."

Not wanting to disappoint such a senior government official, the major said he'd try to get him a look at the wreckage, short of sending a Navy or Air Force aircraft into Brazil to photograph it. Phoning the blockade commander to see if he had any ideas, he was all smiles when he ended the call. "The Navy has an Insitu ScanEagle drone onboard. It's launched by hand from the deck of the ship and will take digital pictures of the wreckage before the Brazilians arrive."

Bradford didn't believe anyone on the Zodiac was alive, knowing that Vilar had come after them with an attack helicopter. Judging from the wreckage, he succeeded. However, he wasn't about to tell Carter that he was making another assumption. Instead, he wanted a picture of the Zodiac wreckage and bodies.

"Will the drone give us clear enough pictures to identify that bodies?"

"Bodies? There won't be any bodies. That branch of the Amazon is teeming with schools of piranhas. The only remains will be the skeletons that litter the bottom."

Bradford was at a loss for words. He knew piranhas were common in South America but didn't equate them to being here. It took fifteen minutes to get the ScanEagle over the debris field, the major able to access its imagery using a link given to him by the ship's captain. The images were sharp and showed numerous bullet holes in the wreckage, which had a Milpro marking on its side. Because of this marking, Bradford was sure this was a the military-grade Zodiac, making the leap that it was used to rescue Cray by the black ops team masquerading as analysts.

Acknowledging that the terrorists met their end on the water, he thanked the major and the Colombian military for their cooperation and promised an FBI commendation for everyone involved. The Colombian Navy ended the blockade of Leticia, and boat traffic in the area returned to normal.

Once Bradford returned to Bogota, he texted Carter, who seemed to accept that Cray and the other members of the White House team who'd destroyed the Cabal and drove him into hiding were dead. After the call, Bradford went to the bar in his hotel and knocked down a few, waiting for the military to call and say that his flight from the El Dorado International Airport to Apiay was ready. From the airbase, he'd take a Gulfstream 550, which the military designated a C-37B, to Washington. Since he considered himself a VIP, he wasn't about to sit in a commercial airliner for the almost ten-hour flight from Bogota to Washington.

"It's gone," Han Li said, looking at the ScanEagle fade into the distance.

"The pilot's idea of riddling the Zodiac with gunfire, and us hiding in the jungle until the wreckage was spotted, was brilliant, even though I had doubts," Moretti admitted.

"With the current carrying the remains of our craft into the center of the water, it's reasonable for anyone to assume we died there by gunfire from the helicopter and our bodies eaten by piranhas."

"In the short time we've been here, we've killed four snakes, two spiders as large as a baseball glove, and many centipedes and tarantulas. How did you two survive without so much as a knife?" Moretti asked, looking at Cray and Sanders.

"Luck, mostly," Sanders said while holding Cray's hand.

"Let's hope some of that rubs off on us and the second part of the pilot's plan works," Bonaquist said.

"What could go wrong?" McGough asked. "All he has to do is find an inflatable at the airbase, fly uninvited another time into Brazil, and put the craft onto the strip of dirt in front of us—which is a third the size of the patch on which we previously parachuted."

"The real challenge will be the drop because the C-17 will need to be at an altitude high enough for the precision parachute placement of the Zodiac. That means the plane will be detectable on Brazilian radar. They'll wonder why this same diplomatic aircraft is continually in this area and may deny permission to use this airspace," Moretti added. "If the pilot disobeys those instructions, they won't shoot it down because it'll cause a diplomatic incident, but they'll send aircraft to see what he's doing. Dropping the inflatable won't be an option if that occurs, and we're stuck in the jungle."

"How do you think he'll get the Zodiac to us?" Shen asked.

"I'm hoping he's more creative than us."

When the C-17 pilot returned to Apiay Airbase, the crew chief went to see if there was an inflatable on the airbase. When he left, the pilot and co-pilot strategized on how they could get approval for a flight plan that took them over nothing but jungle. As if they needed more pressure minutes ago, the pilot received a call from the commander of the 89th saying that the State Department needed the Globemaster the following day to transport crates to Moscow. Because their aircraft was for the exclusive use of the State Department, the commander said he couldn't object to the request, use another C-17, or reschedule the departure time. If he said it was down for maintenance, they might want to see it. Therefore, their plane needed to be back to Andrews within fourteen hours, giving the ground crew barely enough time to load the cargo.

"What do you think?" the co-pilot asked.

"Let's hope the crew chief finds a Zodiac and the base releases it to him. If he comes up empty, we're staying until we find a way to get the team and those they rescued out of that jungle."

Rocha learned something went wrong with Vilar's flight when he received a command-wide notification from the Ministry of Defence that contact was lost with the Aviation Group commander's aircraft. The message stated that because air traffic controllers couldn't contact the Hind, and it couldn't be in the air because of the limited amount of fuel it carried, the Ministry concluded that Vilar's aircraft had gone down.

Calling one of his contacts in the Ministry, he learned Vilar had filed a flight plan and that the focus of the search was the area around Porto Vilho, which was on the Madeira River. Since this city of half a million was notorious for its high crime rate and drug dealing, the military was always sending personnel there to enhance security. Rocha knew Vilar filed to fly to this destination, knowing it wouldn't raise an eyebrow. Staying below radar, he could go instead to the Javari Valley with no one being the wiser. Once he finished speaking with his Ministry contact, he called Bradford.

When Bradford received the call, he was on his way to Apiay Airbase in a Colombian Air Force helicopter. Having had one too many at the bar, he thought he'd misheard Rocha and asked him twice to repeat what he said. He finally got it the third time.

"It's possible he could have destroyed the Zodiac and killed everyone in it before he crashed," Rocha volunteered. "I find it hard to believe they shot down a Hind with ground fire."

"I find it hard to believe that Cray survived a crash, the jungle, a headhunter, a skilled military squad, and was in a US military Zodiac. Yet, that happened."

"Have the Colombian Navy reinstitute the blockade," Rocha suggested.

"On what basis? I don't think the Colombian government would be enthusiastic about again instituting a blockade when I can't offer them proof the terrorists weren't on that Zodiac, not to mention that a second request is likely to make its way back to the Ambassador and possibly the president. That can't happen."

"Then what?" Rocha asked. "If they leave the jungle alive, we're looking at being incarcerated for the rest of our lives. In Brazil, I'll be an embarrassment to the government and the military. They'll kill me, although the official report will say it was suicide. You got me into this; get me out." The call ended.

It was eighty miles from Bogota's El Dorado International Airport to Apiay Airbase. There was a road connecting them, but the poorly maintained strip of asphalt, which had numerous potholes, was notorious for bending wheel rims, causing tire damage, and damaging struts and shocks. Therefore, motorists kept their speed low, causing considerable congestion. Since everyone in Bogota knew this, the agent in charge put Bradford in a military helicopter instead of providing a car and driver.

Thirty minutes after lifting off from the El Dorado International Airport, his helicopter set down near the Gulfstream 550. Fifty yards behind it was the State Department's Globemaster III which, without markings, looked to be another one of the unmarked US military aircraft that punctuated the airbase. Therefore, Bradford didn't give the C-17 a second thought until he saw a Zodiac with a Milpro label loaded into the plane's cargo bay. That caught his attention.

The C-17's crew chief watched as the palleted boat entered the aircraft's hold, telling the forklift operator to set it down just behind the ramp's hinge. Once it was in place, he secured it to the airframe.

"This is a Milpro Zodiac with a JPADS attached to it," the pilot said, looking at the craft in amazement.

"There's a dozen of these in the warehouse. The supply sergeant has been around the block a few times and says they're used extensively by special forces. Since they don't always bring them back undamaged, he keeps a large number in inventory. Half have JPADS."

"How did you get one?"

"I told him the truth and said we have a black ops team stranded on a strip of land in the Amazon and we need to get them another inflatable, but I can't requisition one since their mission never happened. After seeing the Globemaster patch on my flight suit, he said he'd send it to our aircraft. I told him where we were, and here it is."

"He's not expecting it back?" the co-pilot asked.

"He's going to write it off since he never gets questioned why special ops teams don't always return with their Zodiacs."

"That solves one problem?" the pilot said.

"The other?"

"Keeping the Brazilians from seeing us drop this. How strong is your relationship with the supply sergeant?"

"Solid. I think."

"Have him replace the JPADS with a drogue chute. We have a delivery to make."

Bradford was about to board the Gulfstream. Instead, he stopped and watched as the same Zodiac he saw loaded on the C-17 a few minutes earlier was now being brought down the cargo ramp. Curious about what was happening, he boarded the plane but told the pilot that he was delaying their departure for an indeterminant amount of time. Taking a seat on the side of the aircraft facing the Globemaster, he watched to see what would happen next. Thirty minutes later, the Milpro labeled Zodiac returned. Once it was on board, the rear cargo door closed, and the aircraft's giant engines spun up.

Because he didn't believe in coincidence, Bradford found it interesting that the Globemaster would leave with a Zodiac unaccompanied by a team of special operators. That made little sense. What did make sense was the C-17 dropping a replacement for the bullet-ridden craft he saw floating on the water. Assuming Vilar didn't destroy the Zodiac before his aircraft went missing, it was conceivable that Cray and those with him disembarked on shore, shoved the craft into the water, and pumped enough bullets into it to make it seem like someone attacked it. The lack of bodies wasn't an issue, at least to the Colombians, who believed the piranhas devoured them.

"Change of plans; we're going to Leticia," Bradford said as he walked into the cockpit.

The pilot, accustomed to spur-of-the-moment changes on VIP flights, didn't have a problem with a new destination and modified their flight plan. Ten minutes later, both aircraft were airborne and heading in the same direction.

"This water is teeming with hungry piranhas, and we can't get ankle-deep in it before being bloodied. Without a JPADS, how will you get the Zodiac to us?" Moretti asked the pilot, who'd called him once the Globemaster left Apiay. Once again, he had their conversation on speaker.

"I'll be dropping it from a low altitude using a drogue chute."

"That may be a problem. I measured with my GPS the strip of land that we're on. It's three hundred feet long and sixty-five feet wide. What's the length of your wings, from tip to tip?"

"One hundred seventy feet."

"Your wings are twenty feet too long on the jungle side if you're coming in below the treeline, which is around two hundred feet high."

"I have a drogue chute, so we'll be well below that height."

"Have you ever flown a drop like this before?"

"Once."

"How did it turn out?"

"I'll tell you after I release the Zodiac. Since it will hit with gusto, you don't want to be on the bank after I release it."

"Thanks for coming back and risking your ass for us."

Moretti heard the pilot's mic click, his way of saying *you're welcome*.

While Bradford's Gulfstream landed at the Alfredo Vásquez Cobo International Airport in Leticia an hour and ten minutes after leaving Apiay, the C-17 terminated its instrument flight plan ten miles from the airport, telling Colombian air traffic control that it was going to practice low-level maneuvers over the tributary. Although this was an unusual request from an aircraft the size of a Globemaster III, ATC granted it, cautioning that Brazilian airspace was extremely close to their location and to remain on the Colombian side of the border.

One problem in flying low and slow with any aircraft is that the plane tends to be unstable because there's less lift due to a decrease in airflow over the wings. Consequently, it doesn't maneuver well. Also, the slower an aircraft went, the more the pilot needed to increase the angle of attack, or pitch of the plane, to generate lift.

This increased wing angle made the aircraft more susceptible to a stall which, at low altitude, would be catastrophic and put the plane in the ground before the engines responded to the pilot pushing the throttles forward for more power. This lack of response is because a jet engine doesn't increase power immediately. It takes a moment because a lot is happening. Moving the throttles forward increases the fuel flow to speed up the turbines, making the compressors spin faster and moving more compressed air into the combustion chambers. In contrast, because prop aircraft don't have turbines, pushing the throttles forward results in a nearly instantaneous increase in speed.

Therefore, the challenge for the C-17's pilot was to keep the aircraft just over minimum controllable airspeed, weave along a narrow and winding corridor below the height of the jungle canopy, and put the Zodiac on a small patch of ground between the jungle and water by feel—a handful for even the most experienced pilot.

CHAPTER
FOURTEEN

The roar of the C-17's four Pratt & Whitney turbofan engines echoed loudly through the tributary, with the throttle setting putting the plane at just above stall speed. The pilot gently brought the aircraft down to within fifty feet above the water and used ground effect to create a cushion of air between it and the plane as he moved the Globemaster from the center of the waterway to his left until its wing nearly brushed the dense jungle. Even then, with the narrow strip of dirt on which he needed to put the Zodiac in front of him, it was still almost twenty feet to the left. Unless he put the aircraft over it, the pallet on which they secured the boat would end up in the piranha-infested water.

"Hold on tight and get ready to release the craft in five," the pilot said to the crew chief through his mic, the copilot counting down the seconds. When he got to one, he yelled *release*. The crew chief pulled the release lever an instant later, and the palletized Zodiac began leaving the aircraft. As it did, the pilot increased power, banked the plane a fraction to the left, and pulled back slightly on the stick. This aligned it with the narrow drop area and elevated its flight path, so it cleared the giant kapok trees bordering the drop zone, after which the crew chief closed the cargo door.

The pilot leveled the aircraft to keep it below Brazilian radar and maintained this altitude until it entered Colombian airspace, where he informed Colombian ATC that he'd finished practicing low-level maneuvers and requested permission to land at the Leticia airport.

The drogue chute, which pulled the Zodiac from the C-17, only opened long enough to extract it from the plane but did nothing to slow its horizontal and vertical momentum. The pallet hit the narrow patch of dirt at a hundred mph and dug a trench nearly two feet deep in the ground as it slowed, flipping over and stopping a couple of feet from where the jungle touched the water.

The one hundred sixty-three pound inflatable, with a two-hundred-pound motor attached to the rear, could withstand a hard landing. Although large portions of the pallet shattered, the motor had flexible packing material that protected it from getting a scratch, and the Zodiac was undamaged.

Forty-five minutes after the craft left the aircraft, the Zodiac was on the tributary and headed for Leticia.

Bradford wasn't a rocket scientist, but he was smart. Given what he knew about the location of the Zodiac wreckage, he concluded that Cray's only chance of escape was through Leticia, which was on the water and the nearest town to the branch of the Amazon he was on. A Google search showed the waterfront wasn't much; the boats docked there were comparable to what one might see in the Louisiana bayous, except for a gunboat with a Colombian flag hanging from an aft mast.

It was essential that Cray and those with him die in Leticia. That would not be easy since he believed the US military was assisting them, a conclusion he made after seeing the Milpro Zodiac entering the C-17. Further, if that aircraft landed at the Leticia airport, it confirmed that it was there to transport whoever was on the Zodiac to the States, meaning the end of his career and the start of his life in federal prison. Therefore, Cray and those with him must die before getting onto that aircraft. Since a second blockade was out of the question, and he didn't have the expertise to kill a black ops team by himself because he was more a knife in the back type of person, he thought about who in Colombia could ensure Cray and his companion's return to the US would be in coffins. He called Rocha.

"Leticia, Colombia is two miles from Tabatinga, Brazil," Rocha said after Bradford expressed his belief that the Zodiac loaded onto the C-17 was a replacement for the one found on the tributary, its destruction a ruse Cray created to foster the impression that he and those with him died.

"How does that help us? If they get on the C-17, which I believe will land in Leticia to return them to the States, we're both done."

"Because it's a frequent smuggling point for cocaine from Colombia, with whom we share a thousand-mile border, the Federal Police in Colombia and the Brazilian Army work together to keep terrorists and smugglers out. We brand Cray and those with him as terrorists and give their photos to both sides."

"We can't let them take prisoners."

"Both governments have a policy of questioning the lower level people who transport the drugs to learn about their networks and the identities of the higher-ups. However, if those in the police or military are in danger, the gloves come off, and they're permitted to neutralize the threat."

"But they're taken alive if they don't prove dangerous?" Bradford asked.

"Yes," Rocha confirmed.

"I'll wire money to federal officers, soldiers, their family, or anyone else they want if they kill everyone and get rid of the bodies."

"Suggesting that to the colonel in charge of the Tabatinga office would be a mistake. He's a straight arrow and might empty his gun into you if you offer him a bribe."

"We'll stay with the story that they're terrorists trying to sneak into Leticia."

"Which is in Colombia. Any interdiction solely by Brazilian soldiers or police will need to happen on our side of the border."

"Then the colonel will need to intercept them before they get within sight of Leticia."

"I'll call him."

"If he's a straight arrow and won't kill someone he doesn't consider dangerous, how do we ensure everyone dies?"

"That's where you come in."

"What does that mean?"

Rocha explained.

"The C-17 pilot says the State Department moved up their departure time from Joint Base Andrews, and they're going straight back to the States," Moretti said upon ending his satphone call, with McGough at the controls pedal to the metal toward Leticia.

"Does that mean we're flying commercially?" Shen asked.

"I wish. There's a problem with our passports," Moretti replied.

"No immigration stamps," Han Li volunteered.

"Except for Doug and Erin, who legally entered Brazil, the rest of us have no entry stamp into Brazil or any other country. We were supposed to leave the same way we arrived, on a military transport with no questions asked. Colombian immigration at the airport will want to know how we got into the country."

"We look like special forces sent for drug interdiction, especially with our weapons, but I'm uncertain that story will hold once they look under the covers and check with whatever function coordinates US military presence," Bonaquist added. "Looking as grungy as we do, and because we don't have any identifying flags or patches, the Colombians might conclude we're drug smugglers or terrorists."

"Especially with our weapons. We'll have to get rid of them before we reach Leticia," Moretti said. "We can't carry them through town, and we can't explain how we got them if we're intercepted and boarded before docking. As it is, we'll have a tough enough time getting past the lack of passport stamps."

"Colombian customs and immigration would look the other way if we got on the C-17, with or without identifying insignia," Shen added.

"That ship has sailed. Any ideas?"

"Get on another US government aircraft," Bonaquist said.

"How do we find one, let alone get onboard since they can't know who we are?"

"I haven't the vaguest idea."

Colonel Affonso Abreu was the commander of the Traíra Detachment—part of the 1st Border Command of the 1st Special Border Battalion in Tabatinga, Brazil. He was five feet eight inches tall with a dark black mustache, short black hair, and penetrating hazel eyes. At thirty-eight, he was lean and trim and had his share of armed encounters with smugglers and terrorists, the bullet hole scars on his left shoulder, abdomen, and both thighs were a visual testament to those conflicts.

The detachment began operations in Tabatinga forty years ago to confront the lawlessness that occurred from illegal Brazilian and Colombian gold miners. While illegal mining was still a problem, his current focus was on apprehending smugglers, who found the roads and trails near the Amazon town to be an expeditious way to smuggle drugs from Colombia into Brazil.

Rocha's call came as a surprise. The two officers couldn't stand one another and only saw or spoke at staff events or on video conference calls. The reason for this lack of bonding was that Abreu knew Rocha was corrupt because his aide tried to bribe him to look the other way for a large drug shipment through his area. Instead, he took the information the aide gave him, arrested the traffickers, and destroyed the contraband.

Abreu sent a summary of his conversation with Rocha's aide up the chain of command. However, nothing came of it because the aide died in a robbery the night he returned to Brasilia. Subsequently, with no proof the colonel knew anything about the incident, the military hierarchy attributed the attempted bribe to his aide. Because Rocha had an excellent record of job performance, and the Army wasn't going to remove someone of his rank without solid proof, the investigation stopped with the aide taking the fall. A grudge followed, not only because of the accusation and Rocha losing a large amount of money from the confiscation of the shipment, but because Abreu couldn't tolerate anyone who wore the uniform caring more about themselves than their country. Therefore, he answered Rocha's call with a question instead of a greeting.

"What do you want?" Abreu asked.

"I received information that a group of terrorists is in a Zodiac on the Amazon River tributary that passes by Leticia, and that they intend to cross the border into Tabatinga."

"Call the Colombian military; that town is on their side of the tri-border."

"You and I know the Colombian military and police in that border town are a joke. I was hoping you could intercept them while they're still in Brazilian waters so they don't get away."

"What's in this for you?"

"Nothing. I'm doing my duty."

"What's in this for you?" Abreu repeated in a forceful voice. "We both know you could call Vilar and have one of his copters intercept the Zodiac."

"These terrorists shot down his aircraft and killed him."

Abreu didn't know what to say next. The connection between them remained silent until he concluded the call from Rocha could be legitimate. He asked what he knew about the terrorists and their approximate position.

The detachment commander understood he had two choices. The first was to call the head of the small military unit in Leticia and tell him what Rocha said because, once the smugglers set foot on Colombian soil, it would be his problem. The other was intercepting the Zodiac before it entered Colombian waters, as Rocha suggested. He opted for this, deciding it would be easier to confront the terrorists on the water than in the jungle.

The markers delineating the border between Brazil and Colombia were large and on both banks of this branch of the Amazon River. Because Tabatinga and Leticia were so close, the towns historically worked together and ignored the international demarcation between them. They believed the boundary was only meaningful to government and military officials in Brasilia and Bogota and those who lived outside the two towns who didn't know their arrangement.

As part of their relationship, Leticia allowed Abreu's detachment to keep a LAR at its docks, knowing the detachment's use of it in their waters helped keep them safe. Although the boat belonged to the Navy, the detachment operated and maintained it so the Navy wouldn't incur the expense of keeping personnel in Leticia.

Abreu brought seven soldiers with him to the LAR, not worried about how many terrorists were on the Zodiac because of the vessel's firepower. As he and his men arrived at the dock, he saw someone waiting beside the boat, figuring that he was an American because of his facial features and that his clothes were too formal for a jungle environment. The man walked toward him as he approached the vessel and presented his credentials.

"What can I do for the FBI?" Abreu asked as his men boarded the LAR and prepared it for departure.

"Colonel Rocha told me about the terrorists. I want to come along."

"What do you know that I don't?" Abreu asked, not surprised that Rocha hadn't told him everything.

"Everyone but two on the inflatable is American. The Bureau wants to show our involvement when they release news of their apprehension. We could use the good publicity."

"You gave Rocha this information?"

Bradford nodded he did.

Not seeing a downside in bringing along someone from the FBI, he invited him onboard. "Do you have a weapon?" he asked.

"I'd like one."

As they stepped on deck, he asked one of his men for an automatic rifle. Removing it from a bag of weapons, the soldier handed the gun and an ammo magazine to the colonel, who slapped the magazine into the chamber and gave the weapon to Bradford. "The safety is on," Abreu said, pointing to the lever. "I have a firm rule. We only fire when fired upon. Our goal is to capture and interrogate. This is a Brazilian operation; you're an observer, and the gun is only for protection."

"I understand," Bradford said.

"My GPS shows we're four miles from the Colombian border," Moretti said. "Going along with Jack's suggestion, now would be a good time to dump our weapons, magazines, and anything else that reeks of the military into the water."

The team began throwing their weapons and gear over the side. Sixty seconds later, they saw a LAR positioned in the center of the tributary, with its 7.62 mm and 12.7 mm machineguns, a 40 mm grenade launcher, and the automatic weapons of the crew pointed at them. Moretti pulled the throttles back, and the Zodiac coasted toward the LAR.

"Kneel known, lace your fingers on top of your heads, and don't move," they heard someone say in broken English over a megaphone.

They complied.

Bradford's eyes locked on Cray, kneeling beside Sanders at the front of the Zodiac. He had seconds to act, knowing that the inflatable was coasting towards them and everyone inside the Zodiac would soon be a prisoner. He couldn't let Cray speak with Abreu because it would shatter his and Rocha's story. When the colonel discovered he worked for the White House, which meant he and those with him weren't the terrorists they said they were, Abreu would place them under his protection and ensure they returned safely to the US. He couldn't let that happen. The consequences of Cray speaking with the president far outweighed what he was about to do.

When the Zodiac was twenty-five feet from the LAR, he raised his weapon and centered it on Cray's chest. Knowing he couldn't miss at this distance, he planned to put a couple of quick rounds into him and then switch to full auto and kill everyone else in the boat. Flipping the safety off, he adjusted his stance to absorb the kick from the weapon, looked through the gunsight, and began to squeeze the trigger gently.

Visually locking on Cray, he put everything else out of his mind as he pulled the trigger twice. The bullets, traveling at two thousand eight hundred feet per second, hit their target. The first pierced the right lung and pulmonary artery, taking part of them with it as it exited the body. The second round pierced the heart.

CHAPTER
FIFTEEN

E rin Sanders had an eye for detail. Years of photography had ingrained in her the ability to notice minutiae that went unnoticed by others. While the Colombian soldiers on the boat had their guns trained in the Zodiac's direction, their body language showed they didn't expect trouble from an unarmed kneeling group with their fingers laced atop their heads. However, the one person who wasn't in uniform, his facial features and skin tone indicating he wasn't of Latin descent, didn't share that belief. He had his weapon aimed squarely at Cray, the micromovements of his rifle showing he was adjusting his aim and was preparing to shoot. When he flipped the safety off and brought his right leg back an inch, she knew he was going to press the trigger at any instant.

What happened next occurred in a flash—Sanders instinctively shoving Cray onto the deck to get him out of the line of fire. While that saved his life, it took hers. In getting him out of the way, she'd moved into the spot he was in a moment earlier. The two-round burst killed her instantaneously, throwing her body onto Cray, who looked into her lifeless eyes with disbelief and intense agony.

Standing two feet from Bradford, the gunfire startled Abreu. Looking to his right, he saw the FBI intel director moving the lever on his weapon to full auto and adjusting his aim. Realizing what was about to happen, the colonel grabbed the rifle out of his hands and punched him as hard as he could in the face, breaking his nose.

"I told you we only fire if fired upon and that the gun was solely for your protection," he angrily yelled at the unconscious agent. Turning around, he ordered his soldiers to lower their weapons, although most had already done so.

The LAR maneuvered alongside the Zodiac. Abreu and a member of his crew stepped onto it to see if they could save the person the American shot. The amount of blood on Cray and the deck indicated otherwise. The colonel had confronted many terrorists over the years. While he didn't believe those on the Zodiac were tourists, his initial read was that they weren't terrorists. Unsurprisingly, Rocha lied to him.

"Why did you shoot an unarmed person?" Moretti asked Abreu, his anger apparent.

"Believe me when I tell you it was against my orders," he responded in broken English. "Follow me to Leticia, and we'll sort this out." The colonel motioned the crewman with him to return to the LAR, and he followed.

Cray refused to release his embrace of Sanders and openly wept as Moretti followed the LAR. Bradford, who'd regained consciousness, had one set of handcuffs placed on him by Abreu, with another securing those cuffs to the railing. He went into a rant, threatening the Traíra Detachment commander with retribution from the United States government and demanding to be put on a plane back to the States. The colonel, tired of listening to his threats, ordered him to be gagged.

When both crafts docked in Leticia, Abreu put everyone, including Sanders' body, in two military vehicles and drove to the Hospital Militar in Tabatinga. Cray, who refused to leave his fiancé's side, accompanied her gurney to the emergency room, where a nurse drew the curtain to give them privacy.

Bradford, still handcuffed and gagged, remained in the back of a military vehicle to roast in the heat while Abreu's men went into the air-conditioned facility.

"What about him?" one nurse asked the colonel, seeing Bradford had blood caked around his nose. "He could suffocate if he's gagged with a broken nose."

"If he was going to suffocate from a broken nose, he'd already be dead. Leave him. Anyone who tries to help will answer to me."

Not knowing what this person did, the nurse assumed it was terrible and wasn't going to risk her career and possibly her well-being on someone with a broken nose.

The colonel entered the room where those on the Zodiac, minus Cray and Sanders, were sitting. "Who's in charge?" he asked in a respectful voice.

Moretti came forward and introduced himself.

Abreu reciprocated and apologized for what happened, saying the person who killed the woman discharged his weapon against his standing orders. "Can you explain what you were doing in Brazil and what this is about?" he asked Moretti.

""One of your men killed an innocent woman whose only crime was photographing the jungle," Moretti answered, ignoring the question.

"A photographer accompanied by men in jungle camouflage, who look in better physical condition than my soldiers. I suspect there's much more to this story. One of my men didn't kill her; someone from your FBI did. He told me that everyone on your Zodiac were terrorists, which is why we stopped you."

"An FBI agent?"

"Samuel Bradford, the FBI's executive assistant director for intelligence," Abreu said, removing the business card from his pocket and handing it to Moretti.

"I know his name, but I've never seen him before."

"He was targeting the person beside the victim who, intentionally or not, got in front of him."

"His name is Doug Cray, head of the White House Statistical Analysis Division."

"He works for the president of the United States?" Abreu asked, surprised.

"As do we all," Moretti said.

"Can I see your passports?"

Knowing they didn't have a choice, everyone handed them over.

"Greece. A very nice country. I want to go there someday," Abreu said, looking through Moretti's passport first. He quickly scanned the other passports, handing them back when he was through. "I don't see immigration stamps for either Colombia or Brazil."

Moretti didn't answer. Instead, he cleared his throat in response.

"The White House must have quite a physical fitness program. Putting aside that I don't believe the story of White House analysts accompanying someone photographing the Amazon jungle, especially since you were in the military version of a Zodiac," Abreu said, having noticed the Milpro tag on the side of the inflatable, "give me the actual reason you're here. I've worked with American special ops teams in the past. I assume that's your occupation, and your weapons are at the bottom of the tributary."

Moretti made several assumptions that proved to be correct. The first was that the colonel didn't want to arrest them for entering the country illegally and didn't want to become involved in whatever they were doing. The third was that he felt responsible for Sanders' death and wanted to help them. "My explanation will take a while."

"I've got nothing but time. However, I have one thing I need to do first," he said, going into the hallway and telling one of his men to throw a bucket of cold water over Bradford and give him something to drink. "I didn't want such an important person from the FBI to get heat stroke in the middle of your story," he said after translating for Moretti, who followed him into the hallway, what he said to the soldier.

Moretti never mentioned Nemesis, telling the colonel enough so that he could understand the team was here to rescue Cray from a Brazilian death squad sent by Rocha, who was in league with Bradford.

"Rocha is an aquele filho da puta," Abreu said, the Portuguese translation of which was SOB.

"What are your plans for the person from the FBI?"

"He killed a civilian without provocation in Brazilian territory. I'll put him in jail and he can plead his case in court like any other criminal."

"And if I want you to hold him incommunicado in a cell?"

"I'd say that, regrettably, his paperwork for remanding him to civilian authorities got lost and took time to find. Why"

"Can you get Colonel Rocha to come here?"

"When?"

"Within the next week."

"I'll think of something. Now that we agree on what I need to do, what do you have planned?"

Moretti told him.

After Abreu left to transport Bradford to his cell and they took Sanders to the morgue, a nurse brought Cray to the team. He moved slowly, looking in a daze as he sat next to Moretti, the front of his clothes red from his fiancé's blood. Seeing his condition, Han Li left the room and returned several minutes later, handing him a set of green scrubs. He placed them on his lap.

"I took this from the Zodiac," Moretti said, handing Cray his fiancé's camera bag.

He put it on top of the scrubs. "I'm going to take her home to New York," he said, looking at Moretti. "Her parents will hate me for her death."

"You didn't kill her; Bradford did," he replied, explaining what Abreu said about him.

"It wasn't fair that she saved my life. She had everything to live for. I have an empty house, no children, no wife, or anything consequential to show for my time on this planet. That's going to change, starting now. When we return to the States, I'm resigning my commission and recommending the president do away with my position and make you the singular head of Nemesis. Alexson and Connelly can handle the routine administrative BS."

"You're three years from retirement. Call it a day in three years."

"I want to build a life, not a resume. You and Han Li have that. You're all business in the field and kindred spirits at home. I want that closeness only in civilian life and never want to jeopardize the one I love or worry about someone coming after my family or me because of my job. I've given everything I have to my country for the past seventeen years. I'm not getting younger. I want a family before I get too old to enjoy them."

"You deserve one," Moretti said with a smile. "But before then, we need to get a few things out of the way."

Bradford was thrown into a solitary confinement cell in Tabatinga under an assumed name. Abreu didn't record his incarceration, with detachment logs showing his cell was vacant. Once Bradford was in jail, Moretti made several calls. The first was to the commander of the 89th Airlift Wing, asking him when the C-17 aircraft could return to Leticia, indicating his team and a casket needed transport to the States. The colonel didn't ask who the coffin was for nor why he required this huge plane to bring everyone back, believing the reason was that Moretti wanted to confine what the president was doing to a small group of people and didn't want to involve another aircrew.

"The State Department has nothing on their schedule for this aircraft after their current transport. It'll be in Leticia in less than forty-eight hours, barring a last-minute request from State. If you call the pilot, he'll give you a more precise ETA."

Moretti's next call was to Alexson.

"We heard," the techie said before Moretti got a word out.

"Yeah. More on that later. In the meantime, Samuel Bradford has decided to sightsee in the Amazon Basin for a few days. I need you to send an email from him to the acting director telling him he's taking time off."

"Using the FBI's system?"

"Yes. Can you do that?"

"Not a problem."

Moretti's next call was to the C-17 pilot, who said they had already heard from the colonel and would get to Leticia as quickly as possible. "I understand we're returning with a casket," the pilot stated.

"More on that when you get to Leticia. Before then, I need you to stop at Apiay and pick up something. Also, we won't be flying directly to Joint Base Andrews when we leave here. There's someplace we need to go in between."

"I'm not surprised. The aircraft is yours. Let me have you speak with the crew chief, and you can tell him what you need."

The last call was to Abreu, who'd given his cellphone number before returning to detachment headquarters. "Can Rocha be here tomorrow afternoon?" Moretti asked.

"I'll make sure he is?"

"Good. Before then, I'll need a few supplies as soon as possible."

"What are they?"

Moretti told him. "Can you get them?"

"I can. What are they for?"

"I'll tell you when you deliver them."

Getting Colonel Henrique Rocha to Tabatinga was easy once Abreu told him that the lead Bradford gave him resulted in killing seven terrorists, who were devoured by the piranhas when their Zodiac sank in the water. "Since you're responsible for the bust, I thought you should come here for the press conference. If you're unable, I could take your place."

"No," Rocha blurted. "When is the conference?"

Abreu told him.

CHAPTER
SIXTEEN

The C-17 landed at Apiay Airbase and picked up the JPADS that Moretti requested before proceeding to the Leticia airport, parking next to a cargo hangar. Once the pilot shut down the engines, the plane had thirty-five thousand gallons of JP-8 pumped into its fourteen fuel tanks. At the same time, a forklift brought the metal coffin containing Sanders' body into the forward area of the cargo hold, the crew chief securing it with thick nylon straps. He then went into the hangar and affixed the JPADS to the pallet with the supplies that Moretti asked Abreu to bring, walking beside the forklift which brought it onboard. Five minutes later, the Nemesis team stepped up the cargo ramp, Cray conspicuously carrying a thick black marking pen in his right hand. Once onboard, he began drawing on the top and bottom of the plastic packaging covering the supplies.

Bradford was the next to come onboard. Escorted by one of Abreu's men, he was the picture of pompousness as he strutted into the cargo bay.

"When I get back, I'll have warrants issued for your arrests and throw you all in solitary confinement in federal prison. Holding me against my will ensures you get at least twenty years behind bars."

"Don't forget to add the charge for assault," Cray said, punching Bradford on the chin so hard it sent him flying backward onto the deck.

The FBI intel officer was about to say something when McGough put him in a headlock, releasing his hold once he became unconscious.

"Strap him in," Cray said.

As Shen and McGough put Bradford in his harness and zip-tied his hands and feet, Cray took his marking pen and began drawing on his forehead.

Rocha was the last to arrive. Meeting his plane at the Leticia airport, Abreu drove the colonel from the terminal to the hangar behind the C-17.

"Where's the conference?" Rocha asked once they got there.

"There isn't one. You're here for the change in command."

"Which command?"

"Yours," Abreu said, pulling an Axon Taser 7 from the small of his back and sending its two probes into him.

The Taser, set to pulse mode, sent fifty thousand volts of electricity into his central nervous system. This caused neuromuscular incapacitation as the neural signals that controlled his muscles became uncoordinated, resulting in the random contraction of his muscles. Although Rocha was conscious, his coordination was nonexistent for thirty seconds—enough time for Abreu to put his arm around the colonel and get him onboard. When Shen and McGough finished putting him into the harness beside Bradford and zip-tied his hands and feet, Cray approached and began drawing on his forehead.

Moretti walked with Abreu down the ramp, thanking him for everything he'd done. "I owe you," Moretti said. "We couldn't have done this without you."

"Let's call it even. My government got rid of two colonels and a captain and his death squad—all corrupt and out to line their pockets. I don't know what you and your team do for the president, but if anyone asks who was on the Zodiac, I'll tell them you were photographers."

Moretti laughed. Reaching into his pocket, he removed a set of keys and tossed them to him. "For your detachment," he said. "I'm sure you'll have better use for it than taking photographs."

"Adeus meu amigo," Abreu responded before turning around and returning to his vehicle.

After Moretti re-boarded the aircraft, the crew chief closed the cargo ramp. "They look comfortable," he said, staring at the two men in harnesses, both zip-tied, gagged, and attached to the JPADS.

"If you or the pilots have a problem with what we're about to do, tell me now," Moretti said.

"One of your team told me what they did. If that was my fiancé," he said, nodding toward the coffin, "I would put a bullet into each of them and throw their bodies into the Amazon. The pilots feel the same. Where are we taking them?"

"To these coordinates," Moretti said, handing him a slip of paper.

"The same as your last drop."

"Almost. A touch further. I got a GPS fix on this strip of dirt earlier."

"How long is it?"

"Half the size of where you dropped the second Zodiac."

"That won't be a problem with the JPADS. I'll give this to the pilot," he said. "If you don't mind me asking, what's with the drawings on their foreheads?"

Moretti told him.

"I take it back. What you're doing is better than putting a bullet into them," he said, after which he went into the cockpit to hand the pilot the coordinates.

Several minutes later, the C-17 roared down the runway and smoothly lifted into the air. The pilot didn't file a flight plan. Instead, he told the tower he wanted to practice low-level runs along the tributary before activating its IFR flight plan to Dulles. The tower, having heard from ATC that this aircraft had a propensity for practicing low-level runs, acknowledged and approved the request.

The pilot kept the aircraft's speed at one hundred fifty mph and his altitude below two hundred feet to avoid radar detection as he followed the tributary's contortions towards the headhunter's village. Thirty minutes into the flight, Moretti walked into the cockpit. Seeing him, the pilot told the co-pilot that he had the plane.

"How far away are we?" Moretti asked.

"Ten minutes."

"I need this plane to be heard a half a mile inland from where the pallet lands. Will we need to make a pre-drop pass over that area to do that?"

"In case you haven't noticed, this is a noisy aircraft," the pilot said, both men almost shouting to speak to each other. "A mile from the landing zone, I'll put the aircraft into a steep climb, releasing the pallet at two thousand feet. My co-pilot will maneuver the JPADS to your coordinates. At our altitude and power setting, we'll sound like a freight train roaring through the jungle to anyone who's half a mile inland."

"Will any of this be in your flight log?"

"The president has classified this as a top secret/SCI mission. As the originator of your mission, the records and paperwork, if they exist, come from his office and not those downline, such as this aircrew."

"What about your visit to Apiay Airbase?"

"They're special forces central and long ago abandoned keeping records of aircraft arrivals and departures."

"Someone gets the bill for the gas."

"The monthly usage and expense summary for this aircraft is an insignificant number considering the State Department has two hundred six aircraft in its global fleet. Do you think a group of pinstripe-suited bureaucrats are concerned about how much anything costs? Government checks don't bounce because the Department of the Treasury keeps the printing presses running longer. No one's going to notice this aircraft's gas usage."

"Six minutes," the co-pilot said.

"I've got to get back to work."

Moretti left the cockpit.

"My plane," the pilot said, returning his attention to the flight controls and reassuming control of the aircraft.

Moretti walked toward the cargo door and told the team how far they were from the drop zone. On hearing this, Cray removed Bradford's gag.

"You'll spend the rest of your life in jail," Bradford yelled, the noise within the aircraft increasing rapidly as the crew chief opened the cargo door. "When I return to Washington, I'll have you all incarcerated and make your lives a living hell."

"You've already told us. But I don't think you appreciate your position," Cray calmly responded. "In a few minutes, you'll be on a patch of ground a half mile from a village of headhunters. They're generations away from having a phone, if they ever will. And, if you try and escape by going into the water, you won't get five feet from shore before being eaten by piranha."

"That's murder."

"You murdered my fiancé."

"I meant those bullets for you."

"She's still dead. However, in her memory, I'll leave you alone and give you a way out if you tell me where Harrison Carter is hiding."

"I don't know that name."

"How far away are we from the drop?" Cray asked the crew chief, who looked at his watch.

"A little over three minutes."

"I don't know," Bradford screamed.

"Would you mind if I released the pallet?" Cray asked the crew chief, ignoring Bradford.

"It's easy. Pull this lever, and the pallet's gone," he answered.

"All right! He never told me where he was hiding; I only found out by accident. Were you ever in his office in Davos?"

"Get serious."

"On his desk is a cowrie shell. They're widespread in Sri Lanka and the Maldives. Sri Lanka is a lower-to-middle-income country, while the Maldives is luxury personified."

"That narrows his location to over a thousand islands."

"Look for the most luxurious residence, and you'll find him."

"Sixty seconds," the crew chief said as the aircraft gradually began gaining altitude.

"I gave you the information you wanted. Cut me loose."

Rocha, who'd been listening but couldn't speak because they gagged him, was screaming something, but his words were incomprehensible. Cray removed his gag. What followed was a series of expletives aimed at Bradford for trying to save his skin but not including him.

"Thirty seconds."

"We had a deal," Bradford screamed.

"I told you in memory of my wife that I'd leave you alone and give you a way out if you told me where Harrison Carter is hiding. You did. Here's your way out, and I won't bother you again," Cray said, throwing the lever that released the pallet.

"You bastard!" Bradford yelled as the pallet flew out the cargo door, and his and Rocha's screams faded.

The JPADS chute opened, and the co-pilot expertly maneuvered the pallet. Both men were unharmed as it gently touched down in the center of the narrow patch of dirt.

The Shuar tribe was doing what it did every day, gathering food in the unforgiving environment that was their generational home, when they heard an ominous roar from the direction of the water. Grabbing their weapons, and led by Proud Bird, with Shining Anaconda a step behind his father, the men in the tribe ran through the narrow slit of vegetation to the bank of the tributary, arriving a couple of minutes after the JPADS pallet. Bradford and Rocha didn't see the Shuars at first because they approached from behind, and the two men were facing the water. However, once they came into view, both were catatonic with fear, Rocha wetting his pants as he looked at the heads adorning the waists of most of the men.

When Shining Anaconda saw the symbols on the men and the pallet, he knew immediately that both were from Cray because they'd developed this unique symbology to communicate between them. After seeing what he'd written, he relayed Cray's message to his father, the other members of the tribe listening as he spoke.

"These men killed my woman, tried to kill me, and sent the soldiers to kill everyone in your village," the symbols at the top of the pallet read. Those on Bradford's forehead indicated he was the person who'd killed his fiancé, and those on Rocha's said he sent the squad to slaughter the tribe. At the bottom of the pallet was another series of symbols saying what was inside the boxes were gifts from him. Proud Bird ordered Bradford and Rocha to be cut loose and brought to the shabono, along with the boxes, pallet, and JPADS remains.

When the tribal leader finished opening the last box, the tribe looked at a treasure trove of belts, knives, hatchets, machetes, ropes, string, and a dozen other items they would find useful. With sixty of every item, no Shuar would do without, and Proud Bird distributed the bounty.

There was no discussion or vote on what to do with Bradford and Rocha. Since their clothes were useful and the women didn't want to struggle to get the blood out, they stripped both men naked and brought them to the center of the shabono. Shining Anaconda watched as proud Bird approached to claim his head, picking Bradford because he would be a unique addition to his collection. Once he made his selection, he told Shining Anaconda the other was his. Both men immediately stepped forward and, without hesitation, cut Bradford and Rocha's throats in a practiced motion, continuing until the heads were severed. Once they were, they gave them to two older women to begin the laborious process of shrinking them.

CHAPTER
SEVENTEEN

Upon landing at Joint Base Andrews, the Nemesis team, minus Cray, boarded a waiting helicopter to Site R. After cleaning up, Moretti went to Camp David to brief the president, breaking the news that Cray was leaving the military and the reasons for that decision.

"I can station him anywhere he wants for the three years he has remaining until retirement. He doesn't need to throw his career away."

"I'll tell him, sir."

"That said, I won't stand in his way if he still wants to leave."

Moretti knew the military didn't have to accept an officer's resignation of their commission. It could say thanks for sharing and tell the officer they were irreplaceable at present and to get back to work. Although this was rare, he'd seen it happen.

"What about Harrison Carter?" the president asked, getting off the subject of Cray.

"We think he's in the Maldives," he answered, explaining what Bradford told Cray.

"Go after him. Otherwise, he'll send another assassin to kill Cray. Doug won't always be lucky."

"Desperate people will say anything to save their life. Carter may not be in the Maldives."

"You can't overlook that possibility. But wherever he is, even if he's sitting next to Satan in hell, find and kill him."

While Moretti was speaking to the president, Cray arranged for Erin's body to be transported to a mortuary in Greenwich Village, remembering she had told him that her parents lived in Tribecca, which was only a mile away. He decided to notify them of their daughter's death rather than having the police knock on their door. He also needed to give the items she had with her.

Alexson found their address in a government database, and the following morning he drove from Washington to New York City. The drive took five and a half hours, an hour longer than expected because of morning traffic. He intended to tell her parents he was an analyst working for the president, and how they had met at the Manaus charter plane company and shared the same floatplane so that she could capture photographs of illegal logging activities in the Amazon before taking him to his cruise ship.

Editing the rest of their story, he would explain that the plane had a mechanical malfunction and crashed in the jungle, killing the pilot. After barely surviving for days in the rainforest, an Amazonian tribe happened upon them and sent a runner to summon help from a Brazilian military outpost. While together, they fell deeply in love and wanted to get married. The photos on Erin's camera would support that narrative.

He would say that two poachers wandered into their camp while waiting for help to arrive. Because they were carrying jaguar pelts, a protected jungle species, and after hearing that a military rescue party was coming, they began shooting. Although the tribesmen killed them, it wasn't before they murdered their daughter. He felt like a heel for lying, but telling the truth wasn't an option because it would jeopardize Nemesis and the president.

The parents took the news terribly, as he knew they would, initially not believing what he said about their engagement until he handed them their daughter's camera bag, and they looked at her photos. Seeing how happy she looked confirmed that she was engaged to the stranger sitting across from them.

"Where is she now?" the mother asked, tears coming from her eyes and down the sides of her face.

He gave the mortuary's name and location, adding their daughter had been embalmed in Latin America. The parents said they wanted to see her.

"The mortuary may be able to recommend a cemetery close to you if you don't have one in mind."

"We're not burying Erin here," she said. "We have a family crypt in Maine."

"Rockport," Cray responded.

"She told you?"

"Erin said that she eventually wanted to move there. I wasn't told about the family crypt."

"It's in Seaview Cemetery," the father added, in a voice that showed he was trying to hold it together but could come apart at the seams at any moment. "I'll call and see when they can accommodate her internment."

"I can drop you at the mortuary if you like before I drive back to Washington."

"Are you in a hurry?" the mother asked.

"Not in the slightest."

"When's the last time you saw Erin?"

"In the hospital," he replied, remembering holding her lifeless body in the emergency room.

Seeing that his pain mimicked theirs, she invited him to accompany them to the mortuary. "Tonight, you'll sleep in the guest room and come with us tomorrow to Rockport. It's a seven-hour drive from here. We'll take two cars, so afterward you can return to Washington."

"Thank you for inviting me."

"You didn't marry our daughter, but if she wanted to spend the rest of her life with you, then you're family."

Cray broke down and cried.

The internment occurred the following day, with Erin's father having coordinated with the cemetery to get the necessary approvals. The crypt was at the top of a hill and overlooked the water in a view that could appear on the front of a postcard. It could accommodate six coffins, Erin's being the first to be placed inside.

No one planned what happened next. As Cray sat and took in the view, with Erin's parents on both sides of him, they began talking. For the next four hours, they told him about their daughter. Too late to drive back to New York, everyone spent the night at a motel, the parents leaving late the following morning while he returned to Seaview Cemetery to place a bouquet of roses on Erin's grave.

Three days later, Cray returned to Site R and walked into the conference room, where the team was looking at an image on a giant LED screen. On seeing him, someone turned on the lights, the expressions on everyone's faces showing they were glad he was back, if only for a short time. Before anyone could ask a question, heading off any discussion of Erin, the funeral, or the date he would leave the military, he inquired what was on the screen.

"Raa Atoll, the island in the Maldives where we believe Harrison Carter is hiding," Moretti answered.

"The cowrie shell?"

"Bradford was correct about the shell. If you exclude Sri Lanka for the reasons he said, the Maldives is the only country of significance where you can find the cowrie shell. This country is also a non-extradition nation."

"Assuming Bradford wasn't lying, and there was a cowrie shell on Carter's desk," Cray shot back.

"Since we don't know if he was lying about the Maldives, until proven otherwise, we must assume he's hiding there. If there was a shell on his desk, it was decidedly out of place considering the decor of his Swiss residence, because I didn't see any nautical bobble or artwork when I was there," Moretti countered.

"Why Raa Atoll?"

"The Maldives has twelve hundred small coral islands and sandbanks grouped in clusters or atolls. Because Carter requires privacy to maintain his anonymity, let's subtract from that number the atolls and islands with hotels, cottages, or facilities that attract tourists, such as diving venues. We further subtract those with non-opulent residences, as Carter has demonstrated a taste for the good life, and we assume that extends to the tropics."

"And this subtraction has narrowed it down to what's on the screen?"

"Raa Atoll is off-limits to tourists. The residence," Moretti continued, using a laser pointer to put a dot on it, "is forty thousand square feet. Nearby is a helipad, a dock, and an array of satellite and other antennas, making it look like an NSA facility. Moreover, the ownership of this atoll is in the name of an offshore corporation."

"Did the Sentinel take this photograph?" Cray asked, referring to the stealth drone assigned exclusively to Nemesis but on the DOD's books.

"It did," Han Li confirmed. "Daller had it circling above the atoll for almost four hours," she said, referring to the drone's pilot, Major Adam Daller, who piloted the aircraft from Creech Air Force Base in Nevada.

"But it never photographed Carter, or his face would be on the screen."

"We photographed dozens of people, but our facial recognition software never detected him."

"Where's the drone now?"

"Refueling at Diego Garcia, an hour and fifteen minutes away."

"It's your call, Matt. What do you want to do?" Cray asked.

"The other operatives and I comprise the tip of the spear, but you decide when to throw it."

"At least for a few days. I want nothing better than to burst into the residence and see if he's there because I believe you may have found where he lives. However, let's look at this from another perspective."

Everyone on the team respected Cray's ability to analyze a situation.

"If this place belongs to a rich Saudi or Russian oligarch, our raid will be the headline on every news platform in the world because people know there are only a few countries that can conduct this type of operation, the United States being at the top of that list," Cray cautioned. "The Secretary of Defense will take the heat because special ops are under the purview of the DOD."

"That's when everything will unravel," Moretti added.

"Exactly. SecDef will begin an internal investigation to determine if any of the Pentagon's assets were in the area of the Maldives."

"I can't imagine his surprise when he discovers their Sentinel is Diego Garcia gulping gas," Moretti continued. "Since the DOD knows the Statistical Analysis Division of the White House operates it, SecDef will connect the dots between us and our drone being in the area. That's something we can't let happen."

"That's assuming Carter isn't there," Cray said. "He's on the books as a terrorist. If he's there and we kill him, the DOD won't care. Although the public will never hear about it, they'll look no further and take credit for the raid, believing it was one of the alphabet agencies that have a policy of remaining in the shadows. Everyone's happy."

"Therefore, we can't breach the residence and barge in unless we see Carter," Moretti summarized.

"That's what I'm thinking."

"There's another alternative to deploying the Sentinel in four-hour stretches, where it would be easy to miss him, or in breaching the house," Han Li said before explaining what she had in mind.

"Brilliant," Cray responded. "The mission's a go."

It was midnight and moonless when the Dry Combat Submersible, or DCS, silently brought the Nemesis team into the shallow waters of Raa Atoll. The Indian Ocean, which surrounds the Maldives, extends to a depth of over thirteen thousand feet. However, near the atolls, that depth decreases to between one hundred and two hundred sixty feet.

Released off the deck of a Navy sub sixty feet below the surface and ten miles from shore, the DCS took one and a half hours to get to the atoll and settle onto the soft sand thirty feet below the surface, spitting distance from shore. Moretti was the first to leave the diver exit, followed by Han Li, Bonaquist, McGough, and Shen. Although close to the surface, they wore a wetsuit with a hood containing communication equipment in an earphone pocket. Over their suits, each had a rebreather—a closed-circuit system designed not to expel air into the water, and waterproof rucksacks. Night vision goggles, dive fins, and heavy dive boots, which protected them from the sharp coral reefs, completed their gear. The reason for this extensive amount of equipment, even though they could hold their breath to the surface, was in case the DCS needed to move into deeper water to avoid being seen or detected.

They removed their tanks, rucksacks, masks, and fins on reaching the sand. Each had a suppressed Heckler & Koch MK23 .45-cal handgun and a 9mm MP5 submachine gun in their rucksack. The plan was for Moretti and Han Li to enter the residence and kill Carter, if he was there, or leave without being seen while the rest of the team guarded the perimeter.

Moretti and Han Li picked up their rucksacks and slowly approached the residence. Two security guards were visible, one standing outside the front door while the other was in the pool area. Each was alert and had an automatic rifle slung over their shoulder.

"Whoever lives here takes their security seriously. There could be more guards," Han Li cautioned.

"Let's hope not," Moretti responded, holding a device the size of a soap bar in his right hand. The black plastic box had a red and green light. If the green light stayed on, they were fine. If the red light illuminated, there was an active perimeter sensor, which included everything from micro-signals emitted by security cameras to laser trip wires. The signal receptor was sensitive enough to detect emissions before the house's sensors could notice them—at least according to Connelly, who got the device from the DARPA lab. That assumption was put to the test when they'd walked another six steps and the red light illuminated, stopping them in their tracks fifty yards from the house.

"It's time to set the insects free," Moretti whispered.

Han Li took a box out of her rucksack and opened it. Inside were two Black Hornet nano drones and two controllers. Each micro aerial vehicle was four inches long, one inch wide, and weighed just over half an ounce. Capable of reaching a speed of thirteen mph, it could fly or hover for twenty-five minutes.

Both discussed their surprise at seeing open windows, Moretti believing it was because whoever was inside thought they were well-protected by guards and sensors. Han Li's opinion was that the occupants wanted to feel the cool sea breeze and smell the ocean. Both were correct.

""I think we should send the drones through the first open window on the west side of the house," Moretti said.

Han Li agreed.

They sent their drones through the open window and began a systematic search of the house's interior, Han Li's hornet exploring a one hundred eighty-degree arc to the left with Moretti mirroring that search to the right. Two guards patrolled the inside of the residence, but no one else was visible. Six minutes later, they narrowed their search to the room behind a set of double doors in the center and rear of the residence—the only area they hadn't checked.

"That must be the master suite because I didn't see one anywhere else in the house," Han Li said.

"Me either. I think I saw the windows at the rear of the house were open. Let's take the hornets outside and enter through one," Moretti replied.

The window they came through turned out to be the master

suite. It was fifty feet to a side and connected to an enormous bathroom. Sleeping soundly in the king bed were two women in their twenties beside a rotund man in his late fifties or early sixties. He had olive-colored skin, almond-shaped eyes, and coarse hair.

"That isn't the thin man," Moretti said.

"He looks middle-eastern, and the room's decor is an Arab motif."

"We're in the wrong house and possibly the wrong nation. Telling us about the cowrie shell may have been Bradford's way of giving us the finger."

"I don't think so. We're in the right place, but at the wrong time," Han Li said.

"What?"

"Look at the rear of the bedroom."

Moretti maneuvered his drone's camera and focused on the rear wall, made entirely of glass and thirty-five feet in height. "You're right," he said. "It's a duplicate of the front of Carter's mansion in Davos."

"If we had time, I'm sure we'd see other design similarities."

"It doesn't matter. If he's not here, then he's in the wind. Discovering his next hiding place will be like finding a needle in a haystack."

"Maybe not," Han Li said.

CHAPTER
EIGHTEEN

Han Li's idea was to find the manufacturer of the large view windows she and Moretti saw in the Maldives, which was architecturally a duplicate of that in Carter's Davos residence. Although they were in the tropics, where hurricane-resistant glass was common, its thickness was less than half an inch. The windows in the Maldives house were three inches thick, indicating they were bullet-resistant. She believed the chances of a person other than Carter having the same view windows made from bullet-resistant glass was zero.

The team, sitting around her at the conference room table, agreed.

"If he has multiple residences, it's reasonable to assume he'd use the same architect and window manufacturer," Han Li said. "He knows the quality of their work, and they probably have the window and framework specs on file. If we find the company's name and get into their records, we could discover where he's living—assuming he has another architecturally similar residence."

"It's worth a try," Cray said.

They assigned Alexson and Connelly that task. They began with a Google search of how to obtain building permits under Swiss law, discovering that the applicant made a digital submission to the permitting section in the canton where the construction would occur. In contrast, the Maldives had a centralized permitting process with the approval resting with the Ministry of National Planning and Infrastructure.

Once they had this information, the ex-NSA techs had no trouble hacking into the canton and the Ministry's databases, discovering that both residences shared the same architectural firm and bullet-resistant glass manufacturer. Looking at the architect's records, they found that besides the Davos and Maldives mansions, the firm worked on a third house, the techs having to look at a map to find the geographic location of the town and country.

"This country doesn't have an airport," Alexson said, briefing the team on what they discovered.

"Then, what's our plan to get in and out undetected?" Bonaquist asked.

Moretti told him.

"I was afraid you were going to say that."

The principality of Andorra is a sovereign landlocked microstate of mountainous valleys within the southern peaks of the Pyrenees Mountains. It borders Spain to its south and west and France to its north and east. The one hundred eighty-one square mile principality has no railroad nor airport, but it has excellent roads linking it to both countries and a small Spanish airport twelve miles away in Seo de Urgel.

Because there are no customs duties and the taxes are low, the microstate of seventy-seven thousand people attracts millions of shoppers with its duty-free imported goods. Accompanying this robust retail trade is a flourishing banking sector. Lacking an extradition treaty with the United States, and because its consulates are in Barcelona, the microstate has long been a hiding place for those wanting anonymity with relatively easy access to the European continent.

The microstate has seven parishes, the second largest of which is Escaldes-Engordany. The biggest home within this bucolic parish valley had once belonged to a European embezzler who died when his liver succumbed to an over-abundance of duty-free, albeit expensive, alcohol. The thirty-thousand square feet mansion sat at the top of a mountain, the tall windows giving a staggeringly beautiful view of the valley below. Surrounding the plot of land that it was on, which included a helipad, was a ten feet high wall.

"This is getting to be a habit," the pilot of the C-17 aircraft said to Moretti as the Nemesis team, including Cray, walked aboard.

Moretti laughed along with the other team members who, from their facial expressions, became more relaxed upon seeing they had the crew who saved their lives in the Amazon.

"This is not the same aircraft we used in Latin America," Moretti said, seeing that this C-17 had Air Force markings.

"The State Department's aircraft is transporting equipment to Hong Kong. A pilot reported that this C-17 has intermittent stability problems, and we're flight-testing the aircraft to determine what causes the instability. That could take some time."

"Who reported the problem?" Moretti asked.

"I did."

Moretti smiled. "So, there's no problem."

The pilot shook his head in the negative. "The gear you requested is onboard and secured. Am I going to be scraping the ground and weaving my way between trees again, or do you have something different in mind?"

"These are our drop coordinates," Moretti said, handing him a slip of paper.

"Europe. Let's see what we've got," the pilot responded, going to the cockpit and entering the coordinates into the navigation computer. "Escaldes-Engordany, Andorra," he said, butchering the pronunciation. "I'll give you this: you never go anywhere that's dull. Is this one-way or roundtrip?"

"Roundtrip. The flight plan should show your destination as Morón Air Base in southern Spain. Along the way, we'll jump, after which you'll declare a problem with the aircraft and land at the nearest airport. That's twelve miles from our drop point and in Spain. You'll wait for us there."

"What's the name of the airport?"

"Seo de Urgel."

"How do you spell that?"

Moretti told him, and the pilot typed it into his navigation computer, bringing up the airport data.

"It's a forty-one hundred feet long asphalt runway that's ninety-two feet wide!" the pilot exclaimed.

"You told me a C-17 can land and takeoff in thirty-five hundred feet."

"If I set the aircraft down at the very start of that runway, and I mean on the very first inch, I'll have a safety margin of only six hundred feet before I run out of asphalt, which may buckle under the aircraft's weight the instant I touch down."

"That could be a problem," Moretti admitted.

"But not the only one. The width of the runway is ninety feet, which means my wings will extend forty feet on either side of it."

"Does that matter?"

"It does if there's navigation equipment, fuel tanks, and other stationary objects beside the runway, which is common for small airports. Any of those can shear a wing. Also, now that I know where we're going, we'll be landing at night."

"They'll see us if we insert during daylight."

"I understand, but the airport data on my screen shows it's closed after dark. The runway won't be lit."

"You'll have night vision glasses. I need to know if you can land the aircraft there. If you can't, my plan falls apart."

"We'll find a way," the pilot said.

The expressions on the faces of the co-pilot and crew chief, who were listening to their conversation, didn't show they shared that optimism.

"As I've said before, this isn't a quiet plane. We'll attract a lot of attention."

"That's where the in-flight emergency comes in."

"Right. When do you plan to return to the aircraft?"

"Before daybreak."

"Let's hope this mission is easier than Brazil," the pilot said, not knowing how far off that wish would be.

The flight from Joint Base Andrews to Andorra took ten hours, including the air-to-air refueling off the coast of Spain, which the pilot requested because he couldn't refuel at Seo de Urgel. The air was as smooth as glass, and there was a full moon as the aircraft gradually descended. Two minutes from Escaldes-Engordany, the cargo door slowly opened.

Knowing Carter had perimeter alarms surrounding his house in Davos, Moretti assumed there would also be intrusion devices around this residence. Therefore, if they parachuted onto the hundred yards of open grass between the ten feet high walls of the compound and the house, he believed an alarm would sound. Since they would be in the open, being in that area wouldn't be conducive to their survival.

Studying the architectural drawings for the residence, he decided the team would land on the pool area at the rear of the walled estate because it was only a few yards from a rear door into the mansion. This didn't mean it'd be a slam-dunk getting inside because he expected Carter's security to be as robust as in Davos, meaning he'd have cameras and guards everywhere.

A common misconception was that it was easy to kill patrolling guards with a suppressed weapon while parachuting. However, for many reasons, military professionals knew that was often a recipe for disaster. The first was that killing people before boots touched the ground gave away their position and negated the surprise of the attack. Therefore, drawing ground fire while in the air was especially bad. Also, each team member had their weapons secured in a gun case because, if they didn't, it was common they'd break loose during the opening shock. Additionally, they were difficult to access and handle while hanging in a harness. Therefore, the team was defenseless until they landed and extracted their weapons.

Exiting the C-17 aircraft, their parachutes opened smoothly, and they descended at eight and a half feet per minute toward the compound, whose exterior had an abundance of bright security lights. Although they didn't detect any guards, they saw three Belgian Malinois on the vast expanse of grass. Seeing them explained the absence of guards. Beside this grassy area was a helipad, which didn't appear in the architectural drawings, with a helicopter atop it. As they continued to descend, two additional Malinois appeared at the edge of the pool deck.

"Change of plans. We're setting down on the second-floor balcony," Moretti said, referring to a twenty feet wide and fifty feet long railed area with patio furniture on it. He didn't need to mention that overshooting it would put them in the pool area, where they'd become chew toys for the Malinois, nor that the balcony on which they were landing was ten feet narrower than their parachutes.

As a rule, a parachute landing area should be no less than five thousand square feet per four jumpers, with an additional eight hundred square feet for each additional parachutist. The place where the team was setting down was substantially less than those minimums.

The first person to land was Moretti, his chute catching the roof when he touched down. As he released his harness, Han Li set down behind him and Cray behind her, their chutes also catching the roof. After touching down, they removed their weapons from their cases. Although their approaches were silent, there was no way around the sound from the impact of their boots on the balcony nor the noise of the ripping nylon parachutes as they snagged on the overlapping tiles. This caused the vigilant Malinois' to bark, resulting in two guards running from inside the residence to the pool area just as Bonaquist touched down.

Although the guards had automatic weapons, they couldn't get a shot at anyone on the balcony because of its depth and the height of the surrounding railing. However, with Shen and McGough still descending, the guards turned their focus on them. Shen, who was almost on the balcony, landed without being struck by gunfire because the guards couldn't adjust to his descent, and the railing blocked their view of him. McGough was another matter. Visible in the moonlight, a stream of bullets cut through several of the canopy chords. With a loss of control, and perilously hanging from the few chords that connected his harness to the canopy, his chute began gyrating as he steeply banked away from the balcony and impacted the pitched roof.

"Blaine, are you alright?" Moretti asked through his mic.

"Hold on, I'll be right there," McGough responded as he removed the knife from its scabbard and cut the remaining chords to his parachute, which snagged on the peak of the roof. This sent the three hundred five pounds Marine sliding down the tiled roof and onto the balcony with a heavy thud. Shaking his head, he gave a thumbs up as he stood and removed the weapons from his case.

"Game on," Moretti said, the team breaking through the three French doors at the back of the balcony, which they discovered, led to a bedroom that was larger than what they'd seen in the Maldives.

The room, which was dark except for the light coming through the broken doors, was empty.

"Someone left in a hurry," Shen said, looking at the sheets on the king-sized bed, which were tangled, and the comforter on the floor.

However, before anyone could add what they thought, a guard burst into the room. Without the benefit of night vision goggles, which the team was wearing, he was still adjusting to the darkness when Bonaquist sent two rounds into him.

"Let's search the house," Moretti said.

McGough opened the bedroom door and poked his head outside. Almost immediately, a gathering of guards at the bottom of the staircase peppered the door and surrounding walls with gunfire.

"We'll be fish in a barrel if we remain in this room," Shen said.

As he said this, there was the unmistakable sound of a helicopter powering up.

"Carter's getting away," Han Li said.

"Get back on the roof, go to that side of the house, and get into one of those rooms," Moretti said to McGough. "Take Shen with you. We'll keep the guards busy and, if we're lucky, catch them in a crossfire."

When they took off, Moretti opened the door, and the rest of the team began shooting at the guards, none of whom seemed to want to be a hero because no one had started up the stairs.

"They know we're not going anywhere. Which means they'll either outwait us or attack with more than automatic gunfire," Cray said.

As if on cue, a grenade struck outside the room and exploded, the shrapnel unable to penetrate the thick lath and plaster walls.

"Let's keep them occupied while McGough and Shen get in place," Moretti said, looking out the door opening and sending a burst of gunfire toward the guards.

The others alternated doing the same, having the desired effect of focusing the guards on their room and keeping them from lobbing another grenade. Because each team member carried seven 30-round magazines for their Heckler & Koch MP5 submachine guns, six in their rucksack and one in their weapon, they had more than enough ammo to keep the guards from coming up the stairway.

Ten minutes after they left, McGough and Shen laid down a stream of bullets behind the six guards who, seeing they were in a crossfire, put down their guns and raised their hands. The rest of the team rushed down the staircase and, after they searched the guards, Cray removed a bundle of flex ties from his rucksack and tossed them to Bonaquist, telling him to secure their hands and legs.

"Does anyone speak English?" Moretti asked.

Three of the guards said they did. He pointed to one. "Get the dogs into that room and close the door," he said, pointing to it. "We don't want to hurt them, but we will if they attack us."

The guard summoned the dogs in Spanish and took them into the room.

"Is there anyone else on the grounds?"

The guard shook his head. "You killed everyone else."

"Describe the owner of this residence."

The guard precisely described Carter.

"I saw two Suburbans parked in the driveway as I parachuted in. Where are the keys?"

"In the vehicle's cup holders."

Moretti sent Shen and McGough to retrieve the cutes that snagged on the roof, then asked Han Li to remove the guard's identification cards from their wallets and smash their cellphones.

"I'll call the police to free you when we're safely away," Moretti said to the guard. "The story you'll tell is that we spoke Russian and were after your boss. Don't report the car stolen; stick to this story, and you'll never see us again. Any variation, and we'll pay each of you a visit. We know who you are," Moretti concluded, showing he had their ID cards in his hand.

Once the parachutes were in the back of the vehicle, and with Moretti at the wheel, they left the estate, Cray giving directions to the airport using the map on his cellphone. Less than a minute later, Moretti received a call from the pilot of the C-17.

"Are you chasing someone?" the pilot asked.

"The person we're after escaped in a helicopter. Why are you asking?"

"Because a helicopter landed here and, after seeing our plane, the pilot ran like a bat out of hell into the only hangar at this airport, and I got a glimpse of a plane inside."

"We're twenty minutes away. Can you keep him from leaving in either the plane or helicopter? If he gets away, we may never find him again."

"Let me see what I can do," the pilot answered before hanging up.

After telling the co-pilot and crew chief what Moretti said, he explained his plan to prevent the person in the hangar from leaving.

As the pilot started two of the Globemaster's four engines, the hangar door lifted, revealing a Pilatus aircraft. The single-engine turboprop had a two-thousand-mile range.

The Pilatus had just turned over its engine when the C-17 moved in front of the hangar door blocking its exit. As the Globemaster was moving, the co-pilot started the last two engines. Once he blocked the hangar door, the aircraft commander skewed the plane to the left by locking the left brake. After setting the parking brake, he pushed hard on both brake pedals and moved the throttles on his number three and four engines to their full forward position so that all engines were at full thrust—engines always numbered from left to right when viewed from the pilot's seat. Each engine, producing forty thousand pounds of thrust, sent an exhaust wake of over one hundred fifty mph into the helicopter, blowing it over and sending it skidding across the tarmac. After seeing this, the pilot pulled back on the throttles.

"He doesn't seem happy," the co-pilot said, seeing the Pilatus pilot getting out of the turboprop with a handgun and coming toward the Globemaster, motioning for the aircraft to move.

"Let's see if he likes this response," the pilot said as he pushed all four throttles to the stops. With the rapidly increasing thrust, he and the co-pilot again pressed hard on their foot brakes to keep the aircraft from sliding, even with the parking brake set. The hope was that the excruciating high-decibel noise from the engines would cause the person to lower the handgun and back away.

"Can you believe this? He's not moving," the co-pilot remarked in disbelief. "He won't be able to hear for a week, but he won't back off."

"The man's desperate. If we maintain our position, there's no way for him to escape."

"This is new. He's running toward the plane and aiming the gun at you," the co-pilot stated.

"Oh, no," was all the pilot had time to say as their assailant got too close to the number two engine, which was sucking copious amounts of air, and anything else in front of it, into the intake to produce the enormous power the pilot was demanding. There was no resisting the hurricane-like force lifting him off the ground and headfirst into the engine.

CHAPTER
NINETEEN

T he Nemesis team buried their parachutes, rucksacks, weapons, and anything else they felt might cause concern to the Andorran and Spanish border guards if they inspected their vehicle. Afterward, they removed civilian clothes from their rucksacks and changed. No sooner were they on their way to the first border crossing than Moretti received a phone call from the C-17 pilot telling him the sequence of events that led to the death of the person they were chasing.

"Thanks for stopping him. Was there just one person in the helicopter?"

"One."

"I didn't think he knew how to fly, but nothing surprises me about him. I would have thought someone as tall and sleight as him would be careful not to get too close to those massive engines."

"Height and weight don't matter if you step too close to a C-17's engine intake at full power. But I don't think we're on the same page. The person I'm talking about wasn't tall or thin."

"The man we're after is around six feet three inches tall and thin as a rail."

"Five feet five or six, tops."

Moretti slammed on the brakes.

After returning to where they'd buried the gear and digging up their weapons and rucksacks, the team raced back to

Escaldes-Engordany, knowing that Carter had put one over on them by having his pilot take the helicopter to the airport. He would have added to the ruse by leaving the hangar door open, and without an aircraft inside, the impression would be that Carter was again in the wind. That deception would have worked had it not been for the C-17 crew.

"He may have already left the house and is off to his next hiding place," Bonaquist said as Moretti drove as fast as he could on the twisting road to the mansion.

"He's still there. We left so quickly after hearing the helicopter take off that he'll think we believe he's on it and chasing him to the airport," Cray said. "Because we'll need to go through two sets of customs and immigration, he'll also believe he has significant time to take his computer, papers, and other important possessions before abandoning the mansion."

"We'll have our answer in a few minutes," Moretti said.

The gates to the residence were closed when they arrived. Moretti pressed the first button under the rearview mirror on a hunch, and they opened. With no easy way to get past the guards and dogs, both of which he believed were now free; he decided to put their six thousand pounds vehicle through the pair of eight feet tall wooden doors at the front entrance.

"Hold on," Moretti said as he pressed his foot to the floor and crashed the Suburban through the doors, skidding across the foyer before stopping. The impact set off the airbags, but the team shook it off and exited the vehicle with their MP5 submachine guns.

Moretti divided the team. While everyone else looked on the bottom floor, he, Cray, and Han Li would check to see if Carter was upstairs. That was the plan. However, no sooner had he said this than three security guards burst through the side door, with Shen taking them out in rapid succession. The three remaining guards, who were behind them, saw this and reversed direction.

While Moretti and Han Li searched the other upstairs rooms, Cray directed his attention to the master suite. He believed the only explanation for not seeing Carter was that he had a safe room. Going on that assumption, and because he could see that someone was in the bed before the team initially burst into the suite, he believed the safe room was there. Subsequently, he began to methodically search for it.

"I know you're here," Cray said as he turned on the overhead light and looked for telltale signs of a secret room.

He walked around the suite, pressing the wall every six inches to see if he hit a trigger that would expose the safe room entrance. When that got him nowhere, he looked for a switch, reasoning it needed to be where Carter could touch it while in bed and enter the safe room in a flash. That logic worked, finding the inconspicuous button under the edge of the nightstand. Pressing it, a section of wall pulled back and recessed, exposing a steel door.

"Bravo," a voice, which was unmistakably Carter's, said through an unseen speaker. "Again, I underestimated you. I expected you'd follow the helicopter to the airport, believing I was on it and, on finding the hangar door open with no plane inside, think I'd escaped. What gave me away?"

"The height of your pilot."

"How would you know that?"

"I had someone at the airport."

"Something I didn't anticipate."

Cray didn't respond.

"Do you miss her?"

"Who?"

"Your fiancé."

"Every second of every day."

"You know that I'll eventually kill her parents? Don't they live in Tribecca?"

"If you want to kill me, I'm here. It's the pinnacle of cowardice to kill innocents."

"My goals have changed. I want you to live with the pain of her and her parents' deaths."

"I'll kill you before you can harm them."

"How? I've called the police. You and your team should leave before they arrive, or they'll arrest you for murder and a litany of other crimes. You can't get to me."

"Watch me."

"This safe room is impregnable, surrounded by six inches of concrete and rebar with a steel entry door. Turn around; your friends have arrived."

Cray turned and saw that Moretti and Han Li were standing behind him.

"The house is secure. Three guards are dead, three surrendered, and the dogs are back in their room. If the police are coming, we should leave," Moretti said.

"Not without him."

"There may not be enough time to pry him out of there."

"I think I'll open an excellent 1996 Dom Perignon to celebrate you leaving," Carter said.

"It'd better be well-chilled," Cray retorted, walking out of the suite and summoning Bonaquist, Shen, and McGough to the upstairs hallway and telling them what he wanted. Hearing this, Moretti and Han Li also got to work. Within minutes, with the second floor ablaze, Cray returned to the master suite.

"This room is fireproof and has independent power, electricity, and everything else I need to survive," Carter said, seeing on his monitors that part of the second floor was on fire.

"I believe you. But I know the limitations of fireproof safe rooms because my parents have one, and it's also on the second floor. Putting it there comes with constraints because, when the floor collapses in a fire, as this will, your safe room will be on the first floor with a very heavy ceiling and walls on top of it—if you don't suffocate before it drops from the smoke that will come through your outside vents. Then there's the fire's temperature, which will be around eleven hundred degrees Fahrenheit, elevating the temperature of your room to three hundred degrees. I'm giving you a choice. Step out now or roast alive inside that room."

The safe room door opened, and Carter stepped out.

"Get everyone into the Suburban that's outside; we're leaving," Cray told Moretti. "While you're down there, release the guards and tell them to take the dogs and get away from the house before it collapses." Grabbing Carter's arm, he dragged him down the stairs, which went up in flames two minutes later.

"Where to?" Moretti asked once Cray got into the vehicle with Carter.

"We need to rebury our equipment."

"I'll give each of you one hundred million dollars to let me go," Carter said. "You'll never hear from me again."

No one responded.

That amount tripled to three hundred million by the time McGough and Shen removed the small shovels from their rucksacks and began unearthing the loose dirt atop their original hole. When they reached the parachutes, they pulled them out and continued digging deeper, suspecting what else would go into the hole."

"I didn't kill her," Carter said to Cray, the bravado he'd displayed while in the safe room gone.

"You've ordered numerous people to kill me, including Bradford. That he murdered Erin by mistake doesn't mean you're innocent of her death. You're as guilty as if you pulled the trigger."

"Killing me won't bring her back. It will only rob everyone from becoming phenomenally rich?"

"But it will protect Erin's parents because, by your words, you intend to kill them."

"As part of our deal, I'll stay away from them."

Cray ignored the remark. "Look around. We're in a desolate location; you have nothing but the clothes on your back, and your billions are meaningless. Was losing everything by coming after me worth it?"

Carter, who knew he couldn't con Cray and was going to die, thought for a second. "Absolutely. I enjoyed every second."

Cray removed the handgun from his shoulder holster and put a bullet into his head.

Once the dirt was put back into Carter's burial plot and the ground smoothed and raked with fallen branches to hide the hole and their tracks, Moretti called the pilot of the C-17 and told him they'd be there shortly. After showing their forged passports to the Andorran and Spanish border guards, which had the necessary stamps courtesy of the techs, Moretti parked the vehicle beside the demolished helicopter.

"Are we good to go?" the pilot asked as they approached.

Moretti said they were. "Will this plane fly on three engines?" he asked.

"The crew and I have been discussing how we get out of here. Because we're not carrying cargo, this plane can fly with two engines. The problem is the runway length. The loss of one engine increases the takeoff distance by fifteen to twenty percent because of the decrease in total thrust and the drag from the dead engine. This runway is forty-one hundred feet long. Fifteen percent takes the aircraft fifteen feet beyond its takeoff threshold, and twenty percent takes it a hundred feet over it."

"We weren't selling Girl Scout cookies in town. We need to get out of here before the shit hits the fan," Moretti said.

"Let me finish. Because there are no obstructions in the area beyond the runway, we can use ground effect to give us those extra feet. Hopefully," the pilot said.

"I don't know what that means, but let's get out of Dodge."

Everyone quickly got onboard, the pilot starting the three good engines and taxing to the end of the asphalt strip. As he and the co-pilot pressed hard on their footbrakes, he advanced the throttles on the three good engines to the stops, holding firm on the brakes as the plane shook while the thrust from its engines increased.

"Now," the pilot said, he and the co-pilot simultaneously releasing their brakes. The C-17 lurched forward, gaining speed as the co-pilot called the runway markers, which gave the distance remaining until the runway ended.

Because the aircraft commander knew he didn't have enough runway, he pulled back on the stick five hundred feet before the asphalt ended. Although there wasn't enough airspeed to lift the Globemaster into a sustained climb, it was sufficient to get it a few feet off the runway. As the giant plane rose, it wallowed unstably in the air, passing over the end of the runway five feet above the ground while riding on a cushion of air, slowly gaining altitude as the plane accelerated and the airflow over the wings increased.

Once airborne and in a sustained climb, the co-pilot contacted Spanish air traffic control, filing a flight plan to Joint Base Andrews even though Morón Air Base was close. The reason for this decision was that the base's engine maintenance unit would find fragments of a person in the number two engine. Since the crew wanted to avoid the question of how they got there, the aircraft commander decided to return to the States.

When the Globemaster landed at Andrews, and after speaking with the pilot, the base's 89th Airlift Wing commander informed his maintenance supervisor that, during the plane's stability tests, the plane's number two engine ingested a flock of birds. Even though the supervisor knew the birds would need to fly in a single file to miss the number one engine and that the size of the cranium fragment within the engine meant they would have to be as large as a Pterodactyl, he read between the lines and confirmed the wing commander's belief that a flock of birds destroyed the engine.

CHAPTER
TWENTY

Cray met President Ballinger in the Oval Office the morning after landing at Andrews. Seated on couches across from each other, he said that he was resigning from the military for personal reasons and would go to Fort McNair Army Base, three and a half miles from the White House, to complete and sign the necessary paperwork. "Nemesis is mission-capable and will be unaffected by my departure," he reassured Ballinger.

Instead of responding, the president segued to another matter. "I have a pressing problem," he began, "and I need your expertise."

Cray was unprepared for the lack of response to his resignation and, not knowing what to say, didn't respond.

"Less than an hour ago, President Liu told me the Chinese Communist Party is not giving him another term, as he previously believed. When he retires, so will General Chien An—replaced by incoming chairman's appointee. Jian Shen, who Chinese military records show is a military attaché working in DC, will receive a promotion to major and return to China. Since Han Li is legally an American citizen, she'll be unaffected."

"What happens to Nemesis?"

"I have no intention of scrapping it. Instead, its sole focus will be to protect the interests of the United States."

"Can't we have the same arrangement with whoever is replacing President Liu? Their intelligence apparatus and the use of their military bases significantly enhances our global capabilities."

"The CIA told me they've already chosen President Liu's successor and that he's a nationalistic hardliner who's less moderate than President Liu."

"President Liu helped Nemesis protect China from two nuclear detonations that would have destroyed Beijing and Shanghai."

"Because only a dozen people know about that, it never happened."

"You're telling me this because you want me to stay and repurpose Nemesis," Cray responded, reading between the lines.

"I'm making a very selfish request. But I won't stand in your way if you want to resign your commission and return to civilian life. You'll still have my respect and gratitude for what you've done to keep this country safe."

"Would you resign?"

"Given your circumstances, maybe. But I believe I can give you what you're looking for without cutting the umbilical to Nemesis. Whether you recognize it or not, you both need each other."

"You'll need to explain, sir."

"Doug, I selected you as the head of Nemesis because of your unique ability to laser-focus on accomplishing the objective and ignoring the Washington bureaucracy, which has created paralysis by analysis. That focus enabled you to uncover and destroy the Cabal while intelligence agencies were still investigating rumors of its existence. If it wasn't for you, there's a strong possibility we'd have a new world order."

"That was Moretti and the rest of the team, sir. I was in the hospital."

"You laid down the trail for them to follow."

"While I accept Nemesis could use my expertise, I don't see why we need one another."

"That should be obvious. It gives you purpose. I know you, Doug. You don't want to sling papers in corporate America or lobby on behalf of a defense contractor for government contracts. You want to make an impactful difference in protecting this nation. Nemesis gives you purpose. Also, because of the time you've spent together, mutual respect for one another, and near-death experiences, you've become a family."

"When I was with Erin, I loved our feeling of closeness and companionship, realizing that I wanted to experience that every day of my life. I want a family. But knowing she died because someone came after me, how can I ever keep anyone related to me safe with what I do?"

"How will they be safe in this world if you step away?"

Cray didn't immediately respond, thinking about what the president had said.

"Tomorrow, a press release will say that you're transferring from the White House Statistical Analysis Division to the Executive Office of the President. You'll be an advisor, which in Washington-speak means bureaucrat. There are eighteen hundred employees in that office, which should make you very uninteresting to bad guys and take you and your family, if you decide to have one besides Nemesis, out of harm's ways."

"What would I be doing?"

"What you're doing now, except from someplace other than Site R, so the break with the Statistical Analysis Division will appear legitimate. With encrypted video and voice, you'll work from a home office. If you get married, this will allow you to form the closeness and companionship you wanted."

"We'll need to recruit additional members to replace Shen and Chien An, and bring Libby Parra fully into our confidence to increase our intelligence access."

"All of which you can handle. This is a critical juncture for Nemesis, and I need a steady hand on the tiller. Will you stay?"

Cray said he would, and that the president was right about him and Nemesis needing one another.

"Does my home office need to be in the DC area?"

"You can live anywhere in the continental US."

"I've got just the place."

AUTHOR'S NOTES

The idea of Lieutenant Colonel Doug Cray surviving an airplane crash in the Amazon jungle came up while having lunch with my close friend, Scott Cray, to whom this novel is dedicated. We discussed that I didn't lay a glove on him in past manuscripts, agreeing it was time to change that because, if a reader believes the writer won't kill the main character, they'll think I'll always write them out of danger. After that, the tension is gone. If it fits the storyline and advances the plot, any character can end up at either the pearly gates or, if you're a villain, a subterranean location.

To prepare for writing *The Chase,* I extensively researched Amazon rainforests, the creatures inhabiting them, the Javari Valley, weapons, aircraft, and so forth. The information I consulted, some of which I incorporated into my manuscript, is referenced below.

I took liberties with the specs on the UH-60 Black Hawk helicopter, which has a range of three hundred sixty-two miles—more than the distance from Manaus to the illegal logging site and back. Since I needed a rotary aircraft to take down the floatplane, and none had the range I required, I decided to use the Black Hawk because I was familiar with this helicopter, even though the Brazilian Air Force doesn't use it. Colonel Vilar, Colonel Rocha, Captain Torres, and others associated with the Brazilian military are fictional characters and do not represent anyone within the military or government, past or present.

The Vale do Javari, or Javari Valley, exists and is thirty-three thousand square miles—the size of Portugal or Austria. As written, it's the most unexplored area on the planet and has the highest concentration of uncontacted tribes, with entry restricted by the Brazilian government to its indigenous population. Although in northern Brazil on the Peruvian border, some distance from where I had the floatplane crash, I couldn't resist using this mysterious valley in my story.

A rainforest is a tropical woodland with an annual rainfall of at least one hundred inches and lofty broad-leaved evergreen trees that form a continuous canopy. Although I had tree branches interlocking, a few feet separate one canopy from another. Scientists aren't sure why the branches don't touch, but it's thought this separation serves as protection against tree-eating caterpillars and diseases like leaf blight. Information on the five layers of a rainforest (the overstory, the canopy, the understory, the shrub layer, and the forest floor) and the percentage of animal life existing in its trees (fifty to ninety percent) is accurate and taken, as was the information on tree separation, from a July 30, 2012 article by Rhett A. Butler in *Mongabay*. You can find this at (https://rainforests.mongabay.com/0401.htm). The sounds that one encounters in the Amazon were in an April 29, 2016 article by the Amazon Aid Foundation, which you can find at

(https://amazonaid.org/imagining-like-amazon/#:~:text=The%20 rainforest%20is%20teeming%20with,louder%20than%20a%20 military%20jet!).

As stated, the SAS developed a method for inserting someone into the dense jungle by parachute using a long rope to lower them onto the ground when their chute became entangled in a tree canopy. You can find information on this in an article in *ParaData*, which is at (https://www.paradata.org.uk/article/tree-jumping-during-malayan-emergency-1948-1960-22nd-sas).

The satcom communications system used by Torres' team was

a figment of my imagination, although systems similar to the one described exist. The US Defense Advanced Research Projects Agency (DARPA) is working on a project they refer to as SQUIRREL, which stands for SQUad Intelligent Robotic Radio Enhancing Links. This uses flying, climbing, or hybrid robots as radio relays to form a self-positioning three-dimensional mesh communication network supporting small units operating in triple-canopy tropical rainforests. An article by John Keller describes this network. You can find it in the May 11, 2021 edition of *Military + Aerospace Electronics* at

(https://www.militaryaerospace.com/communications/article/ 14203043/robots-communications-jungle).

The floor of a rainforest is not the thick, tangled jungle one sees in movies. Instead, it's relatively clear of vegetation because of the darkness created by the tree canopy. Therefore, according to Rhett A. Butler's April 1, 2019 article in *Mongabay*, (https://rainforests. mongabay.com/05-rainforest-floor.html), a flashlight may be more beneficial than a machete when navigating a rainforest floor. Additionally, the canopy not only blocks sunlight but also dampens the rain so much that someone on the jungle floor may not realize it's raining because the raindrops deflect onto various canopy plants.

As described, the Shuar tribe are headhunters living in the Vale do Javari. However, they reside in eastern Ecuador and northern Peru and not, to the best of anyone's knowledge, in Brazil. The tribe collects heads because they believe it houses a person's soul. Shining Anaconda and Proud Bird are members of an Amazonian tribe, the names taken from research conducted by Chapman University. You can find further information on Amazonian tribal names at

(https://news.chapman.edu/2019/06/06/whats-in-a-name-for-amazonian-tribes-theres-a-connection-to-culture-and-identity/).

I'd always assumed that piranha ate whatever was in the water with it, even its neighbors, if hungry enough. However, after reading an April 8, 2022 article by Jason Roberts in *BYA* (*https://www.buildyouraquarium.com/piranha-care/#:~:text= Tank%20Mates%20for%20Piranha%20Fish&text=Well%2 Dfed%20Red%20Belly%20Piranhas,Dollars%20are%20your%20 safest%20choices.*), I learned that the red-bellied piranhas found in the Amazon Basin exist beside peacock bass, armored catfish, pacu, and silver dollar fish, as stated in my story. However, that coexistence ends when they get hungry and can't find anything else to eat.

In researching how headhunters shrink the heads of their enemies, I came across an article by Rose Eveleth in the March 20, 2013 edition of *Smithsonian Magazine*. The process, which reduces the head to one-third its original size, is too complex and gruesome to be included in the manuscript. However, for those interested, a detailed explanation of the process is at (https://www. smithsonianmag.com/smart-news/how-does-one-actually-shrink-a-head-5994665/#:~:text=Tsantsas%2C%20or%20shrunken%20 head%2C%20are,heads%20cut%20on%20the%20battlefield.).

I took information on how to track someone through the jungle from *The Tactical Tracker Archive*, which gives what a skilled tracker will look for when following someone over various terrains. It amazed me that something as subtle as an inverted vegetation leaf, lighter on the bottom and darker on top, shows that someone inadvertently brushed against the leaf and turned it over. You can find this article at (https://463324730.tripod.com/fm90_5.htm).

The shabono communal living structure I described is typical for the Yanomami tribes of the Amazon rainforest but not the Shuar. The population of the Yanomami, who live in the Amazon rainforest on the border between Venezuela and Brazil, is approximately thirty-five thousand. However, instead of congregating in large communities, they live in an estimated two hundred to two hundred and fifty shabono villages. There is no single leader, and each village is autonomous. In contrast, the estimated Shuar population is between forty and ninety thousand. They live in small villages of up to twenty households, each family living in a single structure. They have no political or social organization above the family level. Because the idea of an indigenous tribe living under one roof fits well with my storyline, I used the Yanomami living arrangements for the Shuars. For more information, please visit (https://socks-studio.com/img/blog/shabono-yanomami-03.jpg).

The NSA's Utah Data Center (UDC) is storing every scrap of information collected over the years by the NSA through its satellites, marine, ground, and airborne systems. This includes communication and electronic data on US citizens, although in 2009 the NSA told the Department of Justice these collections were unintentional and that they no longer do this. The one and a half billion dollars, one million square feet facility that's spread over twenty buildings has supercomputers capable of performing 100,000 trillion calculations per second. According to the August 26, 2020 article by Catherine Armstrong in *Only in Your State*: "whether you're shopping for a toaster on Amazon, or booking a flight online to visit your grandmother in Cleveland, the NSA might have records of your online activity." For more information, please go to (https://www.onlyinyourstate.com/utah/nsa-data-center-ut/) and (https://en.wikipedia.org/wiki/Utah_Data_Center).

As written, the government permits the NSA to monitor Americans' international communications while surveilling targeted foreigners abroad. In doing this, they're allowed to *presume* that prospective surveillance targets are foreigners outside the United States, absent specific information to the contrary, making them fair game for warrantless surveillance even though they may not have a connection to the government's foreign intelligence interests. Under this presumption, the NSA can collect and retain purely domestic communications in their databases. More information on this is at (https://www.aclu.org/fact-sheet/documents-confirm-how-nsas-surveillance-procedures-threaten-americans-privacy#:~:text=1.,surveillance%20targeted%20at%20 foreigners%20abroad.).

When I researched the insects, reptiles, animals, and so forth that one expects to encounter in the Amazon rainforest, I couldn't believe the multitude of dangers someone faces in this environment and tried to convey as much of this as I could in the storyline. One of those dangers is the Brazilian wandering spider, the most venomous arachnid in the world, which prefers to hunt its prey on the ground rather than build a web. You can find more information on Amazon insects at (https://www.natureandculture.org/field-notes/amazon-insects/), (https://www.virtual-rainforest.org/Content/Army-Ants. html), and (https://www.rainforestcruises.com/guides/spiders-of-the-amazon#:~:text=The%20Tarantula&text=Tarantulas%20 are%20the%20largest%20spiders,up%20to%2013%20inches%20 across!).

The Naval Support Detachment, São Paulo, was closed at the request of the Brazilian government in 2017. However, it was a figment of the author's imagination that the closure was because their president promised in his campaign to get rid of all foreign military on their soil and strengthen their armed forces so they would never need to ask a foreign government for protection. I created that narrative because it fit the storyline. It let Nemesis, unable to go to a Brazilian base, covertly parachute into the Javari Valley. It should go without saying that policies and attitudes attributed to the president of Brazil, government and political officials, and those in the military are fictional.

The decompression within the C-17 aircraft is accurate and taken from a May 5, 2018 article by Swayne Martin in *Boldmethod*. Hollywood movies don't show the instant fog that occurs in most depressurizations. However, having undergone altitude training in the Air Force, I can tell you that's what happens. You can find more information on aircraft depressurization at

(https://www.boldmethod.com/blog/lists/2018/05/6-things-that-happen-inside-an-airplane-during-a-rapid-decompression/).

To my knowledge, Joint Base Andrews doesn't have a special ops armory, diplomatic pouches in the kitchen, the alert facility I described, or a C-17 State Department aircraft. I wrote these into the storyline to get Nemesis airborne quickly with the equipment they needed. It became too complicated and slowed the story if I obtained the required mission assets from separate locations. I'll also take a Mea culpa for implying that unnecessary items could be in diplomatic pouches. We all know it's beyond the realm of possibility for this to occur.

The Joint Precision Airdrop System, or JPADS, provides precise, high-altitude delivery of cargo and supplies. It utilizes a parachute decelerator, an autonomous guidance unit, and a load container to maintain a predetermined glide and flight path. The guidance system uses GPS data that wirelessly interfaces with a mission planning module onboard the aircraft, receiving real-time weather data to make computational adjustments. Used at altitudes below twenty-five thousand feet, it allows for a single aerial release to multiple locations. You can find more information on this system at (https://asc.army.mil/web/portfolio-item/cs-css-joint-precision-airdrop-system-jpads/).

In trying to create a unique but plausible way to take down the M-35 Hind before it killed everyone on the Zodiac and brought the Matt Moretti-Han Li series to an end, I thought about my experiences flying jet and prop aircraft, where pilots are focused on avoiding the vortices of large planes. In creating this accident, I used a heavy aircraft climbing at full power, generating substantive lift and wicked vortices to put the Hind into an unrecoverable dive. You can find more information on wind turbulence in a May 22, 2022 article in *Executive Flyers* at (https://executiveflyers.com/wake-turbulence-definition-effects-avoidance/), an article by the National Air and Space Museum, at (https://howthingsfly.si.edu/aerodynamics/vortex-drag), and an advisory circular on wake turbulence issued by the FAA on February 10, 2014, at (https://

www.faa.gov/documentLibrary/media/Advisory_Circular/AC_90-23G.pdf).

As described, Porto Velho is on the Madeira River in northwest Brazil. According to *Numbeo*, it's known within the country for its high level of crime and corruption. More information on the city of Porto Velho is at

(https://www.numbeo.com/crime/in/Porto-Velho-Brazil).

Ground effect is real and increases the lift on an aircraft when the wings are close to the ground or body of water. I kept my explanation short to avoid getting into the technical aspects, which would slow the story. In describing this phenomenon, I used a May 21, 2020 article from OneMonroe Aerospace, which is at

(https://monroeaerospace.com/blog/what-is-the-ground-effect-and-how-does-it-affect-airplanes/).

Samuel Bradford, the executive assistant director for intelligence for the FBI, is a fictional character and not indicative that a past or present person in that position was or is corrupt. The referenced coordination between the Bogota field office and the Colombian military is fictional and done for the sake of the storyline. Continuing with my disclaimers, I created the corrupt persons within the Brazilian military and the death squad to sustain tension and make things interesting. There's no indication that the persons in those positions, past or present, have been or are corrupt. Although past military and political corruption in Brazil are well-documented, today's Brazilian military is viewed favorably by most citizens who are tired of corrupt politicians. Brazil's current president, Jair Bolsonaro, is a former Army captain and his running mate is an outspoken retired Army general. Once in office, the president appointed active-duty and reserve military officers to important civilian posts in his administration. Hopefully, this will put the optics of the Brazilian military in a more accurate light.

The Traíra Detachment of the Brazilian Army, which is part of the 1st Border Command of the 1st Special Border Battalion in Tabatinga, was established in 1990 but is three hundred miles north of Tabatinga on the Traíra River. As written, its original purpose was to confront the lawlessness created by illegal Brazilian and Colombian gold miners. Their role gradually expanded to include drug smugglers. More information, including articles whose data I used, is at (https://en.wikipedia.org/wiki/Operation_Traira), (https://apnews.com/article/5b7e4f6dded748ddb6ab47771bf01d86), and (https://theintercept.com/2022/01/10/brazil-military-power-jair-bolsonaro/).

You might notice that I frequently comment about Congress, noting that, with exceptions, and regardless of the political party or being an independent, they seem to work harder at feathering their nest than working for those who elected them to office. Mine is not a unique position, as this institution only has a seventeen percent approval rating (https://www.statista.com/statistics/207579/public-approval-rating-of-the-us-congress/), less than those who believe in the Tooth Fairy. Therefore, when I compare the monetary motivations of congresspeople to that of my more nefarious characters, there seems to be some element of truth that gives credence to that comparison.

One reason for the country's general distrust of Congress is that they operate under a different set of rules than everyone else—and they don't see any problem with this. There's an illuminating article by Susannah Moyer, (https://www.quora.com/How-do-congressmen-become-millionaires-when-they-only-earn-less-than-200-000-00), that summarizes much of what we already know. For example, insider trading is legal for those in Congress, including not only the stock market but also property and businesses. Also, in passing a spending bill, a congressperson may have included funding that earmarks an area where they own property or a business, the funding significantly increasing the value of what they purchased on the cheap, such as land on which a new road connecting two towns is going. Congresspersons have also paid consulting fees to family members, sometimes into the hundreds of thousands.

President Obama signed a bipartisan bill, the Stop Trading on Congressional Knowledge Act, which banned insider trading for Congress, the executive branch, and their staff. This was done with a significant amount of fanfare and press coverage. However, one year later, without fanfare, President Obama signed a bill reversing large pieces of this law after the Senate and the House passed it in largely empty chambers using the fast-track procedure known as unanimous consent. Indeed, the foxes are watching the hen houses.

I want to offer a sincere Mea culpa to those in both parties of Congress, and independents, who don't feather their nest and give unselfishly of their time. Even though I used a broad brush to paint Congresspeople, I appreciate your efforts in trying to make a better life for your constituents and everyone in this country. I know it's difficult, and thank you for hanging in there.

The Dry Combat Submersible, or DCS, exists and is used by Navy SEALS. Unlike previous submersibles used by these special operators, this has a dry interior, which makes extended missions in colder water possible. With a length of thirty-nine feet and a draft and beam of eight, the fourteen-ton submersible can carry a SEAL team sixty-nine miles at a depth of three hundred thirty feet and a speed of six mph. Although the story had the DCS inserted by submarine, it can also be lowered from a vessel. You can find more information on the DCS in *NavalNews* at (https://www.navalnews.com/naval-news/2020/06/ussocom-reveals-dry-combat-submersible-entering-service-soon/).

The Maldives is a sovereign archipelagic country approximately four hundred seventy miles from the southwest tip of Sri Lanka and India. It consists of twelve hundred small coral islands and sandbanks grouped into twenty-six clusters or atolls. In the early 1970s, it was one of the world's twenty poorest countries, dependent on fishing and trading local goods with neighboring nations. In the 1980s, the government instituted an economic reform that encouraged private sector growth, transforming the country into a world-class tourist destination and increasing its population from one hundred thousand to five hundred forty-four thousand. It's expensive. If decide to go there, you might want to ask your bank loan officer to accompany you.

Raa Atoll exists, is not private, and has several luxury hotels. The atoll has eighty-eight islands, fifteen of which are inhabited. For the sake of the storyline, I made the atoll appear much smaller than its forty-three-mile length and nineteen-mile width. The easiest way to get there is by a forty-five-minute seaplane ride from *Malé*, the Maldives's capital and most populous city. One of the most beautiful and tranquil spots on earth, most of those coming to the atoll snorkel or dive to see the reefs and pelagic fish.

The Black Hornet nano drone exists. Weighing half an ounce and with a flying time of twenty-five minutes, it can transmit live video and HD still images to its operator. A pair of these drones, with support equipment, cost one hundred ninety-five thousand dollars.

I the data for minimum parachute landing areas from the United States Parachute Association, using their level two criteria. You can find this at (https://uspa.org/SIM/7). While I believe the military can parachute onto postage stamp-sized areas, they were understandably vague in publishing how small that area could be. Therefore, I used USPA guidelines. As a former pilot, I don't have any experience jumping from an aircraft—the thought being there is an expectation of having the aircraft return in the same condition they gave it to me. Therefore, and I say this with love, there wasn't much discussion about using a parachute.

ABOUT THE AUTHOR

Alan Refkin has written twelve previous works of fiction and is the co-author of four business books on China, for which he received Editor's Choice Awards for *The Wild Wild East* and *Piercing the Great Wall of Corporate China*. In addition to the Matt Moretti-Han Li action-adventure thrillers, he's written the Mauro Bruno detective series and Gunter Wayan private investigator novels. He and his wife Kerry live in southwest Florida, where he's working on his next Matt Moretti-Han Li novel.

Printed in the United States
by Baker & Taylor Publisher Services